THIS BOOK BELONGS TO

GRIMM'S FAIRY TALES

GRIMM'S FAIRY TALES

with ILLUSTRATIONS by
ARTHUR RACKHAM

FALL RIVER PRESS

New York

FALL RIVER PRESS

New York

An Imprint of Sterling Publishing
387 Park Avenue South
New York, NY 10016

ISBN 978-1-4549-1234-7

Distributed in Canada by Sterling Publishing
c/o Canadian Manda Group, 165 Dufferin Street
Toronto, Ontario, Canada M6K 3H6
Distributed in the United Kingdom by GMC Distribution Services
Castle Place, 166 High Street, Lewes, East Sussex, England BN7 1XU
Distributed in Australia by Capricorn Link (Australia) Pty. Ltd.
P.O. Box 704, Windsor, NSW 2756, Australia

For information about custom editions, special sales, and premium and corporate
purchases, please contact Sterling Special Sales at 800-805-5489 or
specialsales@sterlingpublishing.com.

Manufactured in China

2 4 6 8 10 9 7 5 3 1

www.sterlingpublishing.com

CONTENTS

COLOR PLATES

THE FROG-KING

In old times, when wishing still helped one, there lived a king whose daughters were all beautiful, but the youngest was so beautiful that the sun itself, which has seen so much, was astonished whenever it shone in her face.

Close by the King's castle lay a great dark forest, and under an old lime-tree in the forest was a well. When the day was very warm, the King's child went out into the forest and sat down by the side of the cool fountain, and when she was bored she took a golden ball, and threw it up on high and caught it. This ball was her favorite plaything.

Now it so happened that on one occasion the princess's golden ball did not fall into the little hand which she was holding up for it, but on to the ground beyond, and rolled straight into the water. The King's daughter followed it with her eyes, but it vanished, and the well was deep—so deep that the bottom could not be seen. On this she began to cry, and cried louder and louder, and could not be comforted.

And as she thus lamented some one said to her, "What ails thee, King's daughter? Thou weepest so that even a stone would show pity."

She looked round to the side from whence the voice came, and saw a frog stretching forth its thick, ugly head from the water. "Ah! old water-splasher, is it thou?" said she; "I am weeping for my golden ball, which has fallen into the well."

"Be quiet, and do not weep," answered the frog, "I can help thee, but what wilt thou give me if I bring thy plaything up again?"

"Whatever thou wilt have, dear frog," said she—"My clothes, my pearls and jewels, and even the golden crown which I am wearing."

The frog answered, "I do not care for thy clothes, thy pearls and jewels, or thy golden crown, but if thou wilt love me and let me be thy companion and playfellow, and sit by thee at thy little table, and eat off thy little golden plate, and drink out of thy little cup, and sleep in thy little bed—if thou wilt promise me this I will go down below, and bring thee thy golden ball up again."

"Oh yes," said she, "I promise thee all thou wishest, if thou wilt but bring me my ball back again." She, however, thought, "How the silly frog does talk! He lives in the water with the other frogs, and croaks, and can be no companion to any human being!"

But the frog when he had received this promise, put his head into the water and sank down, and in a short while came swimming up again with the ball in his mouth, and threw it on the grass. The King's daughter was delighted to see her pretty plaything once more, and picked it up, and ran away with it. "Wait, wait," said the frog. "Take me with thee. I can't run as thou canst." But what did it avail him to scream his croak, croak, after her, as loudly as he could? She did not listen to it, but ran home and soon forgot the poor frog, who was forced to go back into his well again.

The next day when she had seated herself at table with the King and all the courtiers, and was eating from her little golden plate, something came creeping splish-splash, splish-splash, up the marble staircase, and when it had got to the top, it knocked at the door and cried, "Princess, youngest princess, open the door for me."

She ran to see who was outside, but when she opened the door, there sat the frog in front of it. Then she slammed the door to, in great haste, sat down to dinner again, and was quite frightened. The King saw plainly that her heart was beating violently, and said, "My child, what art thou so afraid of? Is there perchance a giant outside who wants to carry thee away?"

"Ah, no," replied she. "It is no giant but a disgusting frog."

"What does a frog want with thee?"

"Ah, dear father, yesterday as I was in the forest sitting by the well, playing, my golden ball fell into the water. And because I cried so the frog brought it out again for me, and because he insisted so on it, I promised him he should be my companion, but I never thought he would be able to come out of his water! And now he is outside there, and wants to come in to me."

In the meantime it knocked a second time, and cried,

Princess! youngest princess!
Open the door for me!
Dost thou not know what thou saidst to me
Yesterday by the cool waters of the fountain?
Princess, youngest princess!
Open the door for me!

Then said the King, "That which thou hast promised must thou perform. Go and let him in."

She went and opened the door, and the frog hopped in and followed her, step by step, to her chair. There he sat and cried, "Lift me up beside thee."

She delayed, until at last the King commanded her to do it. When the frog was once on the chair he wanted to be on the table, and when he was on the table he said, "Now, push thy little golden plate nearer to me that we may eat together."

She did this, but it was easy to see that she did not do it willingly. The frog enjoyed what he ate, but almost every mouthful she took choked her.

At length he said, "I have eaten and am satisfied; now I am tired, carry me into thy little room and make thy little silken bed ready, and we will both lie down and go to sleep."

The King's daughter began to cry, for she was afraid of the cold frog which she did not like to touch, and which was now to sleep in her pretty, clean little bed. But the King grew angry and said, "He who helped thee when thou wert in trouble ought not afterwards to be despised by thee."

So she took hold of the frog with two fingers, carried him upstairs, and put him in a corner. But when she was in bed he crept to her and said, "I am tired, I want to sleep as well as thou, lift me up or I will tell thy father."

Then she was terribly angry, and took him up and threw him with all her might against the wall. "Now, thou wilt be quiet, odious frog," said she.

But when he fell down he was no frog but a King's son with beautiful kind eyes. He by her father's will was now her dear companion and husband. Then he told her how he had been bewitched by a wicked witch, and how no one could have delivered him from the well but herself, and that tomorrow they would go together into his kingdom. Then they went to sleep, and next morning when the sun awoke them, a carriage came driving up with eight white

She took hold of the frog with two fingers, carried him upstairs, and put him in a corner

horses, which had white ostrich feathers on their heads, and were harnessed with golden chains, and behind stood the young King's servant faithful Henry.

Faithful Henry had been so unhappy when his master was changed into a frog that he had caused three iron bands to be laid round his heart, lest it should burst with grief and sadness. The carriage was to conduct the young King into his kingdom. Faithful Henry helped them both in, and placed himself behind again, and was full of joy because of this deliverance. And when they had driven a part of the way, the King's son heard a cracking behind him as if something had broken. So he turned round and cried, "Henry, the carriage is breaking."

"No, master, it is not the carriage. It is a band from my heart, which was put there in my great pain when you were a frog and imprisoned in the well."

Again and once again while they were on their way something cracked, and each time the King's son thought the carriage was breaking; but it was only the bands which were springing from the heart of faithful Henry because his master was set free and was happy.

KING THRUSHBEARD

A King had a daughter who was beautiful beyond all measure, but so proud and haughty withal that no suitor was good enough for her. She sent away one after the other, and ridiculed them as well.

Once the King made a great feast and invited thereto, from far and near, all the young men likely to marry. They were all marshalled in a row according to their rank and standing; first came the kings, then the grand-dukes, then the princes, the earls, the barons, and the gentry. Then the King's daughter was led through the ranks, but to every one she had some objection to make; one was too fat: "The wine-cask," she said. Another was too tall: "Long and thin has little in." The third was too short: "Short and thick is never quick." The fourth was too pale: "As pale as death." The fifth too red: "A fighting-cock." The sixth was not straight enough: "A green log dried behind the stove." So she had something to say against every one, but she made herself especially merry over a good king who stood quite high up in the row, and whose chin had grown a little crooked. "Well," she cried and laughed, "he has a chin like a thrush's beak!" and from that time he got the name of King Thrushbeard.

But the old King, when he saw that his daughter did nothing but mock the people, and despised all the suitors who were gathered there, was very angry, and swore that she should have for her husband the very first beggar that came to his doors.

A few days afterwards a fiddler came and sang beneath the windows, trying to earn a small alms. When the King heard him he said, "Let him come up." So the fiddler came in, in his dirty, ragged clothes, and sang before the King and his daughter, and when he had ended he asked for a trifling gift. The King said, "Your song has pleased me so well that I will give you my daughter there, to wife."

The King's daughter shuddered, but the King said, "I have taken an oath to give you to the very first beggar-man, and I will keep it."

All she could say was in vain; the priest was brought, and she had to let herself be wedded to the fiddler on the spot. When that was done the King said, "Now it is not proper for you, a beggar-woman, to stay any longer in my palace, you may just go away with your husband."

The beggar-man led her out by the hand, and she was obliged to walk away on foot with him. When they came to a large forest she asked, "To whom does that beautiful forest belong?"

"It belongs to King Thrushbeard; if you had taken him, it would have been yours."

"Ah, unhappy girl that I am, if I had but taken King Thrushbeard!"

Afterwards they came to a meadow, and she asked again, "To whom does this beautiful green meadow belong?"

"It belongs to King Thrushbeard; if you had taken him, it would have been yours."

"Ah, unhappy girl that I am, if I had but taken King Thrushbeard!"

Then they came to a large town, and she asked again, "To whom does this fine large town belong?"

"It belongs to King Thrushbeard; if you had taken him, it would have been yours."

"Ah, unhappy girl that I am, if I had but taken King Thrushbeard!"

"It does not please me," said the fiddler, "to hear you always wishing for another husband; am I not good enough for you?"

The beggar-man led her out by the hand

At last they came to a very little hut, and she said, "Oh goodness! what a small house; to whom does this miserable, mean hovel belong?"

The fiddler answered, "That is my house and yours, where we shall live together."

She had to stoop in order to go in at the low door. "Where are the servants?" said the King's daughter.

"What servants?" answered the beggar-man; "you must yourself do what you wish to have done. Just make a fire at once, and set on water to cook my supper, I am quite tired."

But the King's daughter knew nothing about lighting fires or cooking, and the beggar-man had to lend a hand himself to get anything fairly done. When they had finished their scanty meal they went to bed; but he forced her to get up quite early in the morning in order to look after the house.

For a few days they lived in this way as well as might be, and came to the end of all their provisions. Then the man said, "Wife, we cannot go on any longer eating and drinking here and earning nothing. You must weave baskets."

He went out, cut some willows, and brought them home. Then she began to weave, but the tough willows wounded her delicate hands. "I see that this will not do," said the man; "you had better spin, perhaps you can do that better."

She sat down and tried to spin, but the hard thread soon cut her soft fingers so that the blood ran down. "See," said the man, "you are fit for no sort of work; I have made a bad bargain with you. Now I will try to make a business with pots and earthenware; you must sit in the market-place and sell the ware."

"Alas," thought she, "if any of the people from my father's kingdom come to the market and see me sitting there, selling, how they will mock me?" But it was of no use, she had to yield unless she chose to die of hunger.

For the first time she succeeded well, for the people were glad to buy the woman's wares because she was good-looking, and they paid her what she asked; many even gave her the money and left the pots with her as well. So they lived on what she had earned as long as it lasted, then the husband bought a lot of new crockery. With this she sat down at the corner of the market-place, and set it out round about her ready for sale. But suddenly there came a drunken hussar galloping along, and he rode right amongst the pots so that they were all broken into a thousand bits. She began to weep, and did not know what to do for fear. "Alas! what will happen to me?" cried she; "what will my husband say to this?" She ran home and told him of the misfortune.

"Who would seat herself at a corner of the market-place with crockery?" said the man. "Leave off crying, I see very well that you cannot do any ordinary work, so I have been to our King's palace and have asked whether they cannot find a place for a kitchen-maid, and they have promised me to take you; in that way you will get your food for nothing."

The King's daughter was now a kitchen-maid, and had to be at the cook's beck and call, and do the dirtiest work. In both her pockets she fastened a little jar, in which she took home her share of the leavings, and upon this they lived. It happened that the wedding of the King's eldest son was to be celebrated, so the poor woman went up and placed herself by the door of the hall to look on. When all the candles were lit, and people, each more beautiful than the other, entered, and all was full of pomp and splendor, she thought of her lot with a sad heart, and cursed the pride and haughtiness which had humbled her and brought her to so great poverty. The smell of the delicious dishes which were being taken in and out reached her, and now and then the servants threw her a few morsels of them: these she put in her jars to take home. All at once the King's son entered, clothed in velvet and silk, with gold chains about his neck. And when he saw the beautiful woman standing by the door he seized her by the hand, and would have danced with her; but she refused and shrank with fear, for she saw that it was King Thrushbeard, her suitor whom she had driven away with scorn. Her struggles were of no avail, he drew her into the hall; but the string by which her pockets were hung broke, the pots fell down, the soup ran out, and the scraps were scattered all about. And when the people saw it, there arose general laughter and derision, and she was so ashamed that she would rather have been a thousand fathoms below the ground.

She sprang to the door and would have run away, but on the stairs a man caught her and brought her back; and when she looked at him it was King Thrushbeard again. He said to her kindly, "Do not be afraid, I and the fiddler who has been living with you in that wretched hovel are one. For love of you I disguised myself so; and I also was the hussar who rode through your crockery. This was all done to humble your proud spirit, and to punish you for the insolence with which you mocked me."

Then she wept bitterly and said, "I have done great wrong, and am not worthy to be your wife."

But he said, "Be comforted, the evil days are past; now we will celebrate our wedding."

Then the maids-in-waiting came and put on her the most splendid clothing, and her father and his whole court came and wished her happiness in her marriage with King Thrushbeard, and the joy now began in earnest. I wish you and I had been there too.

❧

TOM THUMB

There was once a poor peasant who sat in the evening by the hearth and poked the fire, and his wife sat and span.

Then said he, "How sad it is that we have no children! With us all is so quiet, and in other houses it is noisy and lively."

"Yes," replied the wife, and sighed, "even if we had only one, and it were quite small, and only as big as a thumb, I should be quite satisfied, and we would still love it with all our hearts."

Now it so happened that the woman fell ill, and after seven months, gave birth to a child, that was perfect in all its limbs, but no longer than a thumb. Then said they, "It is as we wished it to be, and it shall be our dear child"; and because of its size, they named it Tom Thumb. They did not let it want for food, but the child did not grow taller, but remained as it had been at the first, nevertheless it looked sensibly out of its eyes, and soon showed itself to be a wise and nimble creature, for everything it did turned out well.

One day the peasant was getting ready to go into the forest to cut wood, when he said as if to himself, "How I wish that there was any one who would bring the cart to me!"

"Oh, father," cried Tom Thumb, "I will soon bring the cart, rely on that; it shall be in the forest at the appointed time."

The man smiled and said, "How can that be done, thou art far too small to lead the horse by the reins?"

"That's of no consequence, father, if my mother will only harness it, I shall sit in the horse's ear and call out to him how he is to go." "Well," answered the man, "for once we will try it."

When the time came, the mother harnessed the horse, and placed Tom Thumb in its ear, and then the little creature cried, "Gee up, gee up!"

Then it went quite properly as if with its master, and the cart went the right way into the forest.

It so happened that just as he was turning a corner, and the little one was crying, "Gee up," two strange men came towards him.

"My word!" said one of them, "What is this? There is a cart coming, and a driver is calling to the horse and still he is not to be seen!"

"That can't be right," said the other, "we will follow the cart and see where it stops."

The cart, however, drove right into the forest, and exactly to the place where the wood had been cut. When Tom Thumb saw his father, he cried to him, "Seest thou, father, here I am with the cart; now take me down."

The father got hold of the horse with his left hand and with the right took his little son out of the ear. Tom Thumb sat down quite merrily on a straw, but when the two strange men saw him, they did not know what to say for astonishment. Then one of them took the other aside and said, "Hark, the little fellow would make our fortune if we exhibited him in a large town, for money. We will buy him."

They went to the peasant and said, "Sell us the little man. He shall be well treated with us."

"No," replied the father, "he is the apple of my eye, and all the money in the world cannot buy him from me."

Tom Thumb, however, when he heard of the bargain, had crept up the folds of his father's coat, placed himself on his shoulder, and whispered in his ear, "Father do give me away, I will soon come back again."

Then the father parted with him to the two men for a handsome bit of money. "Where wilt thou sit?" they said to him.

"Oh, just set me on the rim of your hat, and then I can walk backwards and forwards and look at the country, and still not fall down."

They did as he wished, and when Tom Thumb had taken leave of his father, they went away with him. They walked until it was dusk, and then the little fellow said, "Do take me down, I want to come down." The man took his hat off, and put the little fellow on the ground by the wayside, and he leapt and crept about a little between the sods, and then he suddenly slipped into a mouse-hole which he had sought out.

"Good evening, gentlemen, just go home without me," he cried to them, and mocked them. They ran thither and stuck their sticks into the mouse-hole, but it was all lost labor. Tom Thumb crept still farther in, and as it soon became quite dark, they were forced to go home with their vexation and their empty purses.

When Tom Thumb saw that they were gone, he crept back out of the subterranean passage. "It is so dangerous to walk on the ground in the dark," said he; "how easily a neck or a leg is broken!"

Fortunately he knocked against an empty snail-shell. "Thank God!" said he. "In that I can pass the night in safety," and got into it.

Not long afterwards, when he was just going to sleep, he heard two men go by, and one of them was saying, "How shall we contrive to get hold of the rich pastor's silver and gold?"

"I could tell thee that," cried Tom Thumb, interrupting them.

"What was that?" said one of the thieves in fright, "I heard some one speaking."

They stood still listening, and Tom Thumb spoke again, and said, "Take me with you, and I'll help you."

"But where art thou?" "Just look on the ground, and observe from whence my voice comes," he replied.

There the thieves at length found him, and lifted him up. "Thou little imp, how wilt thou help us?" they said.

"A great deal," said he, "I will creep into the pastor's room through the iron bars, and will reach out to you whatever you want to have."

"Come then," they said, "and we will see what thou canst do."

When they got to the pastor's house, Tom Thumb crept into the room, but instantly cried out with all his might, "Do you want to have everything that is here?"

The thieves were alarmed, and said, "But do speak softly, so as not to waken any one!"

Tom Thumb however, behaved as if he had not understood this, and cried again, "What do you want? Do you want to have everything that is here?"

Tom Thumb

The cook, who slept in the next room, heard this and sat up in bed, and listened. The thieves, however, had in their fright run some distance away, but at last they took courage, and thought, "The little rascal wants to mock us." They came back and whispered to him, "Come, be serious, and reach something out to us."

Then Tom Thumb again cried as loudly as he could, "I really will give you everything, just put your hands in."

The maid who was listening, heard this quite distinctly, and jumped out of bed and rushed to the door. The thieves took flight, and ran as if the Wild Huntsman were behind them, but as the maid could not see anything, she went to strike a light. When she came to the place with it, Tom Thumb, unperceived, betook himself to the granary, and the maid, after she had examined every corner and found nothing, lay down in her bed again, and believed that, after all, she had only been dreaming with open eyes and ears.

Tom Thumb had climbed up among the hay and found a beautiful place to sleep in; there he intended to rest until day, and then go home again to his parents. But he had other things to go through. Truly, there is much affliction and misery in this world!

When day dawned, the maid arose from her bed to feed the cows. Her first walk was into the barn, where she laid hold of an armful of hay, and precisely that very one in which poor Tom Thumb was lying asleep. He, however, was sleeping so soundly that he was aware of nothing, and did not awake until he was in the mouth of the cow, who had picked him up with the hay.

"Ah, heavens!" cried he, "how have I got into the fulling mill?" But he soon discovered where he was. Then it was necessary to be careful not to let himself go between the teeth and be dismembered, but he was nevertheless forced to slip down into the stomach with the hay. "In this little room the windows are forgotten," said he, "and no sun shines in, neither will a candle be brought."

His quarters were especially unpleasing to him, and the worst was, more and more hay was always coming in by the door, and the space grew less and less. Then at length in his anguish, he cried as loud as he could, "Bring me no more fodder, bring me no more fodder."

The maid was just milking the cow, and when she heard some one speaking, and saw no one, and perceived that it was the same voice that she had heard in the night, she was so terrified that she slipped off her stool, and spilt the milk. She ran in great haste to her master, and said, "Oh, heavens, pastor, the cow has been speaking!"

"Thou art mad," replied the pastor; but he went himself to the byre to see what was there.

Hardly, however had he set his foot inside when Tom Thumb again cried, "Bring me no more fodder, bring me no more fodder."

Then the pastor himself was alarmed, and thought that an evil spirit had gone into the cow, and ordered her to be killed. She was killed, but the stomach, in which Tom Thumb was, was thrown on the midden. Tom Thumb had great difficulty in working his way; however, he succeeded so far as to get some room, but just as he was going to thrust his head out, a new misfortune occurred. A hungry wolf ran thither, and swallowed the whole stomach at one gulp.

Tom Thumb did not lose courage. "Perhaps," thought he, "the wolf will listen to what I have got to say," and he called to him from out of his stomach, "Dear wolf, I know of a magnificent feast for thee."

"Where is it to be had?" said the wolf.

"In such and such a house; thou must creep into it through the kitchen-sink, and wilt find cakes, and bacon, and sausages, and as much of them as thou canst eat," and he described to him exactly his father's house.

The wolf did not require to be told this twice, squeezed himself in at night through the sink, and ate to his heart's content in the larder. When he had eaten his fill, he wanted to go out again, but he had become so big that he could not go out by the same way. Tom Thumb had reckoned on this, and now began to make a violent noise in the wolf's body, and raged and screamed as loudly as he could.

"Wilt thou be quiet," said the wolf, "thou wilt waken up the people!"

"Eh, what," replied the little fellow, "thou hast eaten thy fill, and I will make merry likewise," and began once more to scream with all his strength.

At last his father and mother were aroused by it, and ran to the room and looked in through the opening in the door. When they saw that a wolf was inside, they ran away, and the husband fetched his ax, and the wife the scythe. "Stay behind," said the man, when they entered the room. "When I have given him a blow, if he is not killed by it, thou must cut him down and hew his body to pieces."

Then Tom Thumb heard his parents, voices and cried, "Dear father, I am here; I am in the wolf's body."

Said the father, full of joy, "Thank God, our dear child has found us again," and bade the woman take away her scythe, that Tom Thumb might not be hurt with it. After that he raised his arm, and struck the wolf such a blow on his head that he fell down dead, and then they got knives and scissors and cut his body open and drew the little fellow forth.

"Ah," said the father, "what sorrow we have gone through for thy sake."

"Yes father, I have gone about the world a great deal. Thank heaven, I breathe fresh air again!"

"Where hast thou been, then?" "Ah, father, I have been in a mouse's hole, in a cow's stomach, and then in a wolf's; now I will stay with you."

"And we will not sell thee again, no, not for all the riches in the world," said his parents, and they embraced and kissed their dear Tom Thumb. They gave him to eat and to drink, and had some new clothes made for him, for his own had been spoiled on his journey.

❧

THE ROBBER BRIDEGROOM

There was once on a time a miller, who had a beautiful daughter, and as she was grown up, he wished that she was provided for, and well married. He thought, "If any good suitor comes and asks for her, I will give her to him."

Not long afterwards, a suitor came, who appeared to be very rich, and as the miller had no fault to find with him, he promised his daughter to him. The maiden, however, did not like him quite so much as a girl should like the man to whom she is engaged, and had no confidence in him. Whenever she saw, or thought of him, she felt a secret horror.

Once he said to her, "Thou art my betrothed, and yet thou hast never once paid me a visit."

The maiden replied, "I know not where thy house is." Then said the bridegroom, "My house is out there in the dark forest."

She tried to excuse herself and said she could not find the way there. The bridegroom said, "Next Sunday thou must come out there to me; I have already invited the guests, and I will strew ashes in order that thou mayst find thy way through the forest."

When Sunday came, and the maiden had to set out on her way, she became very uneasy, she herself knew not exactly why, and to mark her way she filled both her pockets full of peas and lentils. Ashes were strewn at the entrance of the forest, and these she followed, but at every step she threw a couple of peas on the ground. She walked almost the whole day until she reached the middle of the forest, where it was the darkest, and there stood a solitary house, which she did not like, for it looked so dark and dismal. She went inside it, but no one was within, and the most absolute stillness reigned. Suddenly a voice cried,

> Turn back, turn back, young maiden dear,
> 'Tis a murderer's house you enter here.

The maiden looked up, and saw that the voice came from a bird, which was hanging in a cage on the wall. Again it cried,

> Turn back, turn back, young maiden dear,
> 'Tis a murderer's house you enter here.

Then the young maiden went on farther from one room to another, and walked through the whole house, but it was entirely empty and not one human being was to be found. At last she came to the cellar, and there sat an extremely aged woman, whose head shook constantly.

"Can you not tell me," said the maiden, "if my betrothed lives here?"

"Alas, poor child," replied the old woman, "whither hast thou come? Thou art in a murderer's den. Thou thinkest thou art a bride soon to be married, but thou wilt keep thy wedding with death. Look, I have been forced to put a great kettle on there, with water in it, and when they have thee in their power, they will cut thee to pieces without mercy, will cook thee, and eat thee, for they are eaters of human flesh. If I do not have compassion on thee, and save thee, thou art lost."

Thereupon the old woman led her behind a great hogshead where she could not be seen. "Be as still as a mouse," said she, "do not make a sound, or move, or all will be over with thee. At night, when the robbers are asleep, we will escape; I have long waited for an opportunity."

Hardly was this done, than the godless crew came home. They dragged with them another young girl. They were drunk, and paid no heed to her

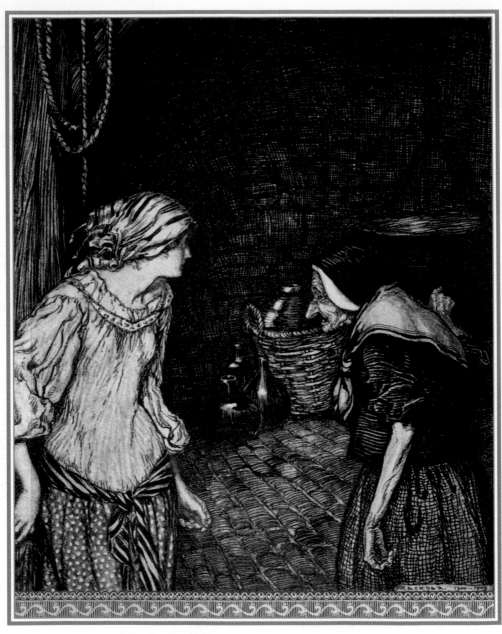

She came to the cellar, and there sat an extremely aged woman,
whose head shook constantly

screams and lamentations. They gave her wine to drink, three glasses full, one glass of white wine, one glass of red, and a glass of yellow, and with this her heart burst in twain. Thereupon they tore off her delicate raiment, laid her on a table, cut her beautiful body in pieces, and strewed salt thereon. The poor bride behind the cask trembled and shook, for she saw right well what fate the robbers had destined for her.

One of them noticed a gold ring on the little finger of the murdered girl, and as it would not come off at once, he took an ax and cut the finger off, but it sprang up in the air, away over the cask and fell straight into the bride's bosom. The robber took a candle and wanted to look for it, but could not find it. Then another of them said, "Hast thou looked behind the great hogshead?" But the old woman cried, "Come and get something to eat, and leave off looking till the morning, the finger won't run away from you."

Then the robbers said, "The old woman is right," and gave up their search, and sat down to eat, and the old woman poured a sleeping-draught in their wine, so that they soon lay down in the cellar, and slept and snored.

When the bride heard that, she came out from behind the hogshead, and had to step over the sleepers, for they lay in rows on the ground, and great was her terror lest she should waken one of them. But God helped her, and she got safely over. The old woman went up with her, opened the doors, and they hurried out of the murderers' den with all the speed in their power. The wind had blown away the strewn ashes, but the peas and lentils had sprouted and grown up, and showed them the way in the moonlight. They walked the whole night, until in the morning they arrived at the mill, and then the maiden told her father everything exactly as it had happened.

When the day came when the wedding was to be celebrated, the bridegroom appeared, and the miller had invited all his relations and friends. As they sat at table, each was bidden to relate something. The bride sat still, and said nothing. Then said the bridegroom to the bride, "Come, my darling, dost thou know nothing? Relate something to us like the rest."

She replied, "Then I will relate a dream. I was walking alone through a wood, and at last I came to a house, in which no living soul was, but on the wall there was a bird in a cage which cried,

> Turn back, turn back, young maiden dear,
> 'Tis a murderer's house you enter here.

They walked the whole night

"And this it cried once more. My darling, I only dreamt this. Then I went through all the rooms, and they were all empty, and there was something so horrible about them! At last I went down into the cellar, and there sat a very very old woman, whose head shook; I asked her, 'Does my bridegroom live in this house?' She answered, 'Alas poor child, thou hast got into a murderer's den, thy bridegroom does live here, but he will hew thee in pieces, and kill thee, and then he will cook thee, and eat thee.' My darling, I only dreamt this. But the old woman hid me behind a great hogshead, and, scarcely was I hidden, when the robbers came home, dragging a maiden with them, to whom they gave three kinds of wine to drink, white, red, and yellow, with which her heart broke in twain. My darling, I only dreamt this. Thereupon they pulled off her pretty clothes, and hewed her fair body in pieces on a table, and sprinkled them with salt. My darling, I only dreamt this. And one of the robbers saw that there was still a ring on her little finger, and as it was hard to draw off, he took an ax and cut it off, but the finger sprang up in the air, and sprang behind the great hogshead, and fell in my bosom. And there is the finger with the ring!" And with these words she drew it forth, and showed it to those present.

The robber, who had during this story become as pale as ashes, leapt up and wanted to escape, but the guests held him fast, and delivered him over to justice. Then he and his whole troop were executed for their infamous deeds.

CINDERELLA

The wife of a rich man fell sick, and as she felt that her end was drawing near, she called her only daughter to her bedside and said, "Dear child, be good and pious, and then the good God will always protect thee, and I will look down on thee from heaven and be near thee." Thereupon she closed her eyes and departed. Every day the maiden went out to her mother's grave, and wept, and she remained pious and good. When winter came the snow spread a white sheet over the grave, and when the spring sun had drawn it off again, the man had taken another wife.

The woman had brought two daughters into the house with her, who were beautiful and fair of face, but vile and black of heart. Now began a bad time for the poor stepchild.

"Is the stupid goose to sit in the parlor with us?" said they. "He who wants to eat bread must earn it; out with the kitchen-wench."

They took her pretty clothes away from her, put an old gray bedgown on her, and gave her wooden shoes.

"Just look at the proud princess, how decked out she is!" they cried, and laughed, and led her into the kitchen. There she had to do hard work from morning till night, get up before daybreak, carry water, light fires, cook and wash. Besides this, the sisters did her every imaginable injury—they mocked her and emptied her peas and lentils into the ashes, so that she was forced to sit and pick them out again. In the evening when she had worked till she was weary she had no bed to go to, but had to sleep by the fireside in the ashes. And as on that account she always looked dusty and dirty, they named her Cinderella.

It happened that the father was once going to the fair, and he asked his two stepdaughters what he should bring back for them. "Beautiful dresses," said one. "Pearls and jewels," said the second.

"And thou, Cinderella," said he, "what wilt thou have?"

"Father, break off for me the first branch which knocks against your hat on your way home."

So he bought beautiful dresses, pearls and jewels for his two step-daughters, and on his way home, as he was riding through a green thicket, a hazel twig brushed against him and knocked off his hat. Then he broke off the branch and took it with him. When he reached home he gave his stepdaughters the things which they had wished for, and to Cinderella he gave the branch from the hazel-bush. Cinderella thanked him, went to her mother's grave and planted the branch on it, and wept so much that the tears fell down on it and watered it. It grew, however, and became a handsome tree. Thrice a day Cinderella went and sat beneath it, and wept and prayed, and a little white bird always came on the tree, and if Cinderella expressed a wish, the bird threw down to her what she had wished for.

It happened, however, that the King appointed a festival which was to last three days, and to which all the beautiful young girls in the country were invited, in order that his son might choose himself a bride. When the two stepsisters heard that they too were to appear among the number, they were delighted, called Cinderella and said, "Comb our hair for us, brush our shoes and fasten our buckles, for we are going to the festival at the King's palace."

Cinderella obeyed, but wept, because she too would have liked to go with them to the dance, and begged her stepmother to allow her to do so. "Thou go, Cinderella!" said she; "Thou art dusty and dirty and wouldst go to the festival? Thou hast no clothes and shoes, and yet wouldst dance!"

As, however, Cinderella went on asking, the stepmother at last said, "I have emptied a dish of lentils into the ashes for thee, if thou hast picked them out again in two hours, thou shalt go with us."

The maiden went through the back-door into the garden, and called,

> You tame pigeons, you turtle-doves,
> and all you birds beneath the sky,
> come and help me to pick
> The good into the pot,
> The bad into the crop.

Then two white pigeons came in by the kitchen-window, and afterwards the turtle-doves, and at last all the birds beneath the sky, came whirring and crowding in, and alighted amongst the ashes. And the pigeons nodded with their heads and began pick, pick, pick, pick, and the rest began also pick, pick, pick, pick, and gathered all the good grains into the dish. Hardly had one hour passed before they had finished, and all flew out again.

Then the girl took the dish to her stepmother, and was glad, and believed that now she would be allowed to go with them to the festival. But the stepmother said, "No, Cinderella, thou hast no clothes and thou canst not dance; thou wouldst only be laughed at." And as Cinderella wept at this, the stepmother said, "If thou canst pick two dishes of lentils out of the ashes for me in one hour, thou shalt go with us." And she thought to herself, "That she most certainly cannot do." When the stepmother had emptied the two dishes of lentils amongst the ashes, the maiden went through the back-door into the garden and cried,

> You tame pigeons, you turtle-doves,
> and all you birds beneath the sky,
> come and help me to pick
> The good into the pot,
> The bad into the crop.

Then two white pigeons came in by the kitchen-window, and afterwards the turtle-doves, and at length all the birds beneath the sky, came whirring and crowding in, and alighted amongst the ashes. And the doves nodded with their heads and began pick, pick, pick, pick, and the others began also pick, pick, pick, pick, and gathered all the good seeds into the dishes, and before half an hour was over they had already finished, and all flew out again. Then the maiden carried the dishes to the stepmother and was delighted, and believed that she might now go with them to the festival. But the stepmother said, "All this will not help thee; thou goest not with us, for thou hast no clothes and canst not dance; we should be ashamed of thee!" On this she turned her back on Cinderella, and hurried away with her two proud daughters.

As no one was now at home, Cinderella went to her mother's grave beneath the hazel-tree, and cried,

> Shiver and quiver, little tree,
> Silver and gold throw down over me.

Then the bird threw a gold and silver dress down to her, and slippers embroidered with silk and silver. She put on the dress with all speed, and

She put on the dress with all speed, and went to the festival

went to the festival. Her stepsisters and the stepmother however did not
know her, and thought she must be a foreign princess, for she looked so
beautiful in the golden dress. They never once thought of Cinderella, and
believed that she was sitting at home in the dirt, picking lentils out of the
ashes. The prince went to meet her, took her by the hand and danced with
her. He would dance with no other maiden, and never left loose of her hand,
and if any one else came to invite her, he said, "This is my partner."

She danced till it was evening, and then she wanted to go home. But the
King's son said, "I will go with thee and bear thee company," for he wished to
see to whom the beautiful maiden belonged. She escaped from him, however,
and sprang into the pigeon-house.

The King's son waited until her father came, and then he told him that
the stranger maiden had leapt into the pigeon-house. The old man thought,
"Can it be Cinderella?" and they had to bring him an ax and a pickax that he
might hew the pigeon-house to pieces, but no one was inside it.

And when they got home Cinderella lay in her dirty clothes among
the ashes, and a dim little oil-lamp was burning on the mantle-piece, for
Cinderella had jumped quickly down from the back of the pigeon-house
and had run to the little hazel-tree, and there she had taken off her beautiful
clothes and laid them on the grave, and the bird had taken them away again,
and then she had placed herself in the kitchen amongst the ashes in her
gray gown.

Next day when the festival began afresh, and her parents and the
stepsisters had gone once more, Cinderella went to the hazel-tree and said—

Shiver and quiver, little tree,
Silver and gold throw down over me.

Then the bird threw down a much more beautiful dress than on the
preceding day. And when Cinderella appeared at the festival in this dress,
every one was astonished at her beauty. The King's son had waited until she
came, and instantly took her by the hand and danced with no one but her.
When others came and invited her, he said, "She is my partner."

When evening came she wished to leave, and the King's son followed
her and wanted to see into which house she went. But she sprang away from
him, and into the garden behind the house. Therein stood a beautiful tall

tree on which hung the most magnificent pears. She clambered so nimbly between the branches like a squirrel that the King's son did not know where she was gone.

He waited until her father came, and said to him, "The stranger-maiden has escaped from me, and I believe she has climbed up the pear-tree."

The father thought, "Can it be Cinderella?" and had an ax brought and cut the tree down, but no one was on it. And when they got into the kitchen, Cinderella lay there amongst the ashes, as usual, for she had jumped down on the other side of the tree, had taken the beautiful dress to the bird on the little hazel-tree, and put on her gray gown.

On the third day, when the parents and sisters had gone away, Cinderella went once more to her mother's grave and said to the little tree—

> Shiver and quiver, little tree,
> Silver and gold throw down over me.

And now the bird threw down to her a dress which was more splendid and magnificent than any she had yet had, and the slippers were golden.

And when she went to the festival in the dress, no one knew how to speak for astonishment. The King's son danced with her only, and if any one invited her to dance, he said, "She is my partner."

When evening came, Cinderella wished to leave, and the King's son was anxious to go with her, but she escaped from him so quickly that he could not follow her. The King's son had, however, used a stratagem, and had caused the whole staircase to be smeared with pitch, and there, when she ran down, had the maiden's left slipper remained sticking. The King's son picked it up, and it was small and dainty, and all golden. Next morning, he went with it to the father, and said to him, "No one shall be my wife but she whose foot this golden slipper fits."

Then were the two sisters glad, for they had pretty feet. The eldest went with the shoe into her room and wanted to try it on, and her mother stood by. But she could not get her big toe into it, and the shoe was too small for her. Then her mother gave her a knife and said, "Cut the toe off; when thou art Queen thou wilt have no more need to go on foot." The maiden cut the toe off, forced the foot into the shoe, swallowed the pain, and went out to the King's son. Then he took her on his horse as his bride and rode away with her. They were, however, obliged to pass the grave, and there, on the hazel-tree, sat the two pigeons and cried,

> Turn and peep, turn and peep,
> There's blood within the shoe,
> The shoe it is too small for her,
> The true bride waits for you.

Then he looked at her foot and saw how the blood was streaming from it. He turned his horse round and took the false bride home again, and said she was not the true one, and that the other sister was to put the shoe on. Then this one went into her chamber and got her toes safely into the shoe, but her heel was too large. So her mother gave her a knife and said, "Cut a bit off thy heel; when thou art Queen thou wilt have no more need to go on foot." The maiden cut a bit off her heel, forced her foot into the shoe, swallowed the pain, and went out to the King's son. He took her on his horse as his bride, and rode away with her, but when they passed by the hazel-tree, two little pigeons sat on it and cried,

> Turn and peep, turn and peep,
> There's blood within the shoe,
> The shoe it is too small for her,
> The true bride waits for you.

He looked down at her foot and saw how the blood was running out of her shoe, and how it had stained her white stocking. Then he turned his horse and took the false bride home again.

"This also is not the right one," said he, "have you no other daughter?"

"No," said the man, "there is still a little stunted kitchen-wench which my late wife left behind her, but she cannot possibly be the bride."

The King's son said he was to send her up to him; but the mother answered, "Oh, no, she is much too dirty, she cannot show herself!" He absolutely insisted on it, and Cinderella had to be called.

She first washed her hands and face clean, and then went and bowed down before the King's son, who gave her the golden shoe. Then she seated herself on a stool, drew her foot out of the heavy wooden shoe, and put it into the slipper, which fitted like a glove. And when she rose up and the

King's son looked at her face he recognized the beautiful maiden who had danced with him and cried, "That is the true bride!" The stepmother and the two sisters were terrified and became pale with rage; he, however, took Cinderella on his horse and rode away with her. As they passed by the hazel-tree, the two white doves cried,

> Turn and peep, turn and peep,
> No blood is in the shoe,
> The shoe is not too small for her,
> The true bride rides with you,

and when they had cried that, the two came flying down and placed themselves on Cinderella's shoulders, one on the right, the other on the left, and remained sitting there.

When the wedding with the King's son had to be celebrated, the two false sisters came and wanted to get into favor with Cinderella and share her good fortune. When the betrothed couple went to church, the elder was at the right side and the younger at the left, and the pigeons pecked out one eye of each of them. Afterwards as they came back, the elder was at the left, and the younger at the right, and then the pigeons pecked out the other eye of each. And thus, for their wickedness and falsehood, they were punished with blindness as long as they lived.

⦅❧⦆

RUMPELSTILTSKIN

Once there was a miller who was poor, but who had a beautiful daughter. Now it happened that he had to go and speak to the King, and in order to make himself appear important he said to him, "I have a daughter who can spin straw into gold."

The King said to the miller, "That is an art which pleases me well; if your daughter is as clever as you say, bring her tomorrow to my palace, and I will try what she can do."

And when the girl was brought to him he took her into a room which was quite full of straw, gave her a spinning-wheel and a reel, and said, "Now set to work, and if by tomorrow morning early you have not spun this straw into gold during the night, you must die." Thereupon he himself locked up the room, and left her in it alone.

So there sat the poor miller's daughter, and for the life of her could not tell what to do; she had no idea how straw could be spun into gold, and she grew more and more miserable, until at last she began to weep.

But all at once the door opened, and in came a little man, and said, "Good evening, Mistress Miller; why are you crying so?"

"Alas!" answered the girl, "I have to spin straw into gold, and I do not know how to do it."

"What will you give me," said the manikin, "if I do it for you?"

"My necklace," said the girl.

The little man took the necklace, seated himself in front of the wheel, and "whirr, whirr, whirr," three turns, and the reel was full; then he put another on, and whirr, whirr, whirr, three times round, and the second was full too. And so it went on until the morning, when all the straw was spun, and all the reels were full of gold.

By daybreak the King was already there, and when he saw the gold he was astonished and delighted, but his heart became only more greedy. He had the miller's daughter taken into another room full of straw, which was much larger, and commanded her to spin that also in one night if she valued her life.

The girl knew not how to help herself, and was crying, when the door again opened, and the little man appeared, and said, "What will you give me if I spin that straw into gold for you?"

"The ring on my finger," answered the girl. The little man took the ring, again began to turn the wheel, and by morning had spun all the straw into glittering gold.

But all at once the door opened and in came a little man

The King rejoiced beyond measure at the sight, but still he had not gold enough; and he had the miller's daughter taken into a still larger room full of straw, and said, "You must spin this, too, in the course of this night; but if you succeed, you shall be my wife." ("Even if she be a miller's daughter," thought he, "I could not find a richer wife in the whole world.")

When the girl was alone the manikin came again for the third time, and said, "What will you give me if I spin the straw for you this time also?"

"I have nothing left that I could give," answered the girl.

"Then promise me, if you should become Queen, your first child."

"Who knows whether that will ever happen?" thought the miller's daughter; and, not knowing how else to help herself in this strait, she promised the manikin what he wanted, and for that he once more span the straw into gold.

And when the King came in the morning, and found all as he had wished, he took her in marriage, and the pretty miller's daughter became a Queen.

A year after, she had a beautiful child, and she never gave a thought to the manikin. But suddenly he came into her room, and said, "Now give me what you promised."

The Queen was horror-struck, and offered the manikin all the riches of the kingdom if he would leave her the child. But the manikin said, "No, something that is living is dearer to me than all the treasures in the world."

Then the Queen began to weep and cry, so that the manikin pitied her. "I will give you three days' time," said he, "if by that time you find out my name, then shall you keep your child."

So the Queen thought the whole night of all the names that she had ever heard, and she sent a messenger over the country to inquire, far and wide, for any other names that there might be. When the manikin came the next day, she began with Caspar, Melchior, Balthazar, and said all the names she knew, one after another; but to every one the little man said, "That is not my name."

On the second day she had inquiries made in the neighborhood as to the names of the people there, and she repeated to the mannikin the most uncommon and curious. "Perhaps your name is Shortribs, or Sheepshanks, or Laceleg?"

But he always answered, "That is not my name."

On the third day the messenger came back again, and said, "I have not been able to find a single new name, but as I came to a high mountain at the

Round about the fire quite a ridiculous little man was jumping:
he hopped upon one leg, and shouted

end of the forest, where the fox and the hare bid each other good night, there I saw a little house, and before the house a fire was burning, and round about the fire a quite ridiculous little man was jumping: he hopped upon one leg, and shouted—

Today I bake, tomorrow brew,
The next I'll have the young Queen's child.
Ha! glad am I that no one knew
That Rumpelstiltskin I am styled.

You may think how glad the Queen was when she heard the name! And when soon afterwards the little man came in, and asked, "Now, Mistress Queen, what is my name?"

At first she said, "Is your name Conrad?"

"No."

"Is your name Harry?"

"No."

"Perhaps your name is Rumpelstiltskin?"

"The devil has told you that! the devil has told you that!" cried the little man, and in his anger he plunged his right foot so deep into the earth that his whole leg went in; and then in rage he pulled at his left leg so hard with both hands that he tore himself in two.

❦

RAPUNZEL

There were once a man and a woman who had long in vain wished for a child. At length the woman hoped that God was about to grant her desire. These people had a little window at the back of their house from which a splendid garden could be seen, which was full of the most beautiful flowers and herbs. It was, however, surrounded by a high wall, and no one dared to go into it because it belonged to an enchantress who had great power and who was dreaded by all the world.

One day the woman was standing by this window and looking down into the garden, when she saw a bed which was planted with the most beautiful rampion, known as rapunzel. It looked so fresh and green that she longed for it, and had the greatest desire to eat some. This desire increased every day, and as she knew that she could not get any of it, she quite pined away, and looked pale and miserable.

Then her husband was alarmed, and asked, "What aileth thee, dear wife?"

"Ah," she replied, "if I can't get some of the rampion, which is in the garden behind our house, to eat, I shall die."

The man, who loved her, thought, "Sooner than let thy wife die, bring her some of the rampion thyself, let it cost thee what it will."

In the twilight of the evening, he clambered down over the wall into the garden of the enchantress, hastily clutched a handful of rampion, and took it to his wife. She at once made herself a salad of it, and ate it with much relish. She, however, liked it so much—so very much, that the next day she longed for it three times as much as before. If he was to have any rest, her husband must once more descend into the garden. In the gloom of evening, therefore, he let himself down again; but when he had clambered down the wall he was terribly afraid, for he saw the enchantress standing before him.

"How canst thou dare," said she with angry look, "to descend into my garden and steal my rampion like a thief? Thou shalt suffer for it!"

"Ah," answered he, "let mercy take the place of justice, I only made up my mind to do it out of necessity. My wife saw your rampion from the window, and felt such a longing for it that she would have died if she had not got some to eat."

Then the enchantress allowed her anger to be softened, and said to him, "If the case be as thou sayest, I will allow thee to take away with thee as much rampion as thou wilt, only I make one condition: thou must give me the child which thy wife will bring into the world; it shall be well treated, and I will care for it like a mother."

The man in his terror consented to everything, and when the woman was brought to bed, the enchantress appeared at once, gave the child the name of Rapunzel, and took it away with her.

Rapunzel grew into the most beautiful child beneath the sun. When she was twelve years old, the enchantress shut her into a tower, which lay in a forest, and had neither stairs nor door, but quite at the top was a little window. When the enchantress wanted to go in, she placed herself beneath it and cried,

He was terribly afraid, for he saw the enchantress standing before him

> Rapunzel, Rapunzel,
> Let down thy hair to me.

Rapunzel had magnificent long hair, fine as spun gold, and when she heard the voice of the enchantress she unfastened her braided tresses, wound them round one of the hooks of the window above, and then the hair fell twenty ells down, and the enchantress climbed up by it.

After a year or two, it came to pass that the King's son rode through the forest and went by the tower. Then he heard a song, which was so charming that he stood still and listened. This was Rapunzel, who in her solitude passed her time in letting her sweet voice resound. The King's son wanted to climb up to her, and looked for the door of the tower, but none was to be found. He rode home, but the singing had so deeply touched his heart, that every day he went out into the forest and listened to it. Once when he was thus standing behind a tree, he saw that an enchantress came there, and he heard how she cried,

> Rapunzel, Rapunzel,
> Let down thy hair.

Then Rapunzel let down the braids of her hair, and the enchantress climbed up to her. "If that is the ladder by which one mounts, I will for once try my fortune," said he, and the next day when it began to grow dark, he went to the tower and cried,

> Rapunzel, Rapunzel,
> Let down thy hair.

Immediately the hair fell down and the King's son climbed up.

At first Rapunzel was terribly frightened when a man such as her eyes had never yet beheld came to her; but the King's son began to talk to her quite like a friend, and told her that his heart had been so stirred that it had let him have no rest, and he had been forced to see her.

Then Rapunzel lost her fear, and when he asked her if she would take him for her husband, and she saw that he was young and handsome, she thought, "He will love me more than old Dame Gothel does"; and she said

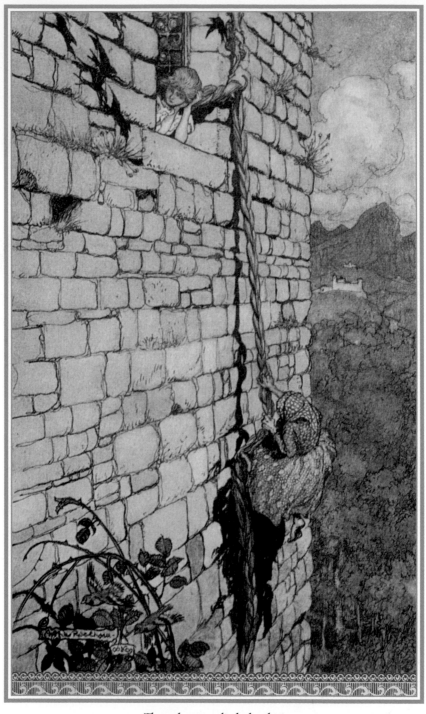

The enchantress climbed up by it

yes, and laid her hand in his. She said, "I will willingly go away with thee, but I do not know how to get down. Bring with thee a skein of silk every time that thou comest, and I will weave a ladder with it, and when that is ready I will descend, and thou wilt take me on thy horse."

They agreed that until that time he should come to her every evening, for the old woman came by day. The enchantress remarked nothing of this, until once Rapunzel said to her, "Tell me, Dame Gothel, how it happens that you are so much heavier for me to draw up than the young King's son—he is with me in a moment."

"Ah! thou wicked child," cried the enchantress. "What do I hear thee say! I thought I had separated thee from all the world, and yet thou hast deceived me!"

In her anger she clutched Rapunzel's beautiful tresses, wrapped them twice round her left hand, seized a pair of scissors with the right, and snip, snap, they were cut off, and the lovely braids lay on the ground. And she was so pitiless that she took poor Rapunzel into a desert where she had to live in great grief and misery.

On the same day, however, that she cast out Rapunzel, the enchantress in the evening fastened the braids of hair which she had cut off, to the hook of the window, and when the King's son came and cried,

> Rapunzel, Rapunzel,
> Let down thy hair

she let the hair down. The King's son ascended, but he did not find his dearest Rapunzel above, but the enchantress, who gazed at him with wicked and venomous looks.

"Aha!" she cried mockingly, "thou wouldst fetch thy dearest, but the beautiful bird sits no longer singing in the nest; the cat has got it, and will scratch out thy eyes as well. Rapunzel is lost to thee; thou wilt never see her more."

The King's son was beside himself with pain, and in his despair he leapt down from the tower. He escaped with his life, but the thorns into which he fell, pierced his eyes. Then he wandered quite blind about the forest, ate nothing but roots and berries, and did nothing but lament and weep over the loss of his dearest wife.

Thus he roamed about in misery for some years, and at length came
to the desert where Rapunzel, with the twins to which she had given birth,
a boy and a girl, lived in wretchedness. He heard a voice, and it seemed so
familiar to him that he went towards it, and when he approached, Rapunzel
knew him and fell on his neck and wept. Two of her tears wetted his eyes and
they grew clear again, and he could see with them as before.

He led her to his kingdom where he was joyfully received, and they lived
for a long time afterwards, happy and contented.

THE STRAW, THE COAL, AND THE BEAN

In a village dwelt a poor old woman who had gathered together a dish of
beans and wanted to cook them. So she made a fire on her hearth, and that
it might burn the quicker, she lighted it with a handful of straw. When she
was emptying the beans into the pan, one dropped without her observing
it, and lay on the ground beside a straw, and soon afterwards a burning coal
from the fire leapt down to the two.

Then the straw said, "Dear friends, from whence do you come here?"

The coal replied, "I fortunately sprang out of the fire, and if I had not
escaped by main force, my death would have been certain—I should have
been burnt to ashes."

The bean said, "I too have escaped with a whole skin, but if the old
woman had got me into the pan, I should have been made into broth
without any mercy, like my comrades."

"And would a better fate have fallen to my lot?" said the straw. "The old
woman has destroyed all my brethren in fire and smoke; she seized sixty of
them at once, and took their lives. I luckily slipped through her fingers."

"But what are we to do now?" said the coal.

"I think," answered the bean, "that as we have so fortunately escaped
death, we should keep together like good companions, and lest a new mis-
chance should overtake us here, we should go away together, and repair
to a foreign country."

The proposition pleased the two others, and they set out on their way
in company. Soon, however, they came to a little brook, and as there was no

In a village dwelt a poor old woman

bridge or foot-plank, they did not know how they were to get over it. The straw hit on a good idea, and said, "I will lay myself straight across, and then you can walk over on me as on a bridge."

The straw therefore stretched itself from one bank to the other, and the coal, who was of an impetuous disposition, tripped quite boldly on to the newly-built bridge. But when she had reached the middle, and heard the water rushing beneath her, she was, after all, afraid, and stood still, and ventured no farther. The straw, however, began to burn, broke in two pieces, and fell into the stream. The coal slipped after her, hissed when she got into the water, and breathed her last.

The bean, who had prudently stayed behind on the shore, could not but laugh at the event, and was unable to stop. She laughed so heartily that she burst. It would have been all over with her, likewise, if, by good fortune, a tailor who was traveling in search of work, had not sat down to rest by the brook. As he had a compassionate heart he pulled out his needle and thread, and sewed her together. The bean thanked him most prettily, but as the tailor used black thread, all beans since then have a black seam.

THE MOUSE, THE BIRD, AND THE SAUSAGE

Once upon a time a mouse, a bird, and a sausage became companions, kept house together, lived well and happily with each other, and wonderfully increased their possessions. The bird's work was to fly every day into the forest and bring back wood. The mouse had to carry water, light the fire, and lay the table, and the sausage had to cook. When the bird came home and laid his burden down, they sat down to dinner, and after they had had their meal, they slept their fill till next morning, and that was a splendid life.

Alas, he who is too well off is always longing for something new. One day, therefore, the bird met with another bird, on the way, to whom it related its excellent circumstances and boasted of them. The other bird, however, called it a poor simpleton for his hard work, but said that the two at home

*The mouse had to carry water, light the fire, and lay the table,
and the sausage had to cook*

had good times. For when the mouse had made her fire and carried her
water, she went into her little room to rest until they called her to lay the
table. The sausage stayed by the pot, saw that the food was cooking well and,
when it was nearly time for dinner, it rolled itself once or twice through the
broth or vegetables and then they were buttered, salted, and ready.

Next day the bird, prompted by the other bird, would go no more into
the wood, saying that he had been servant long enough, and had been made a
fool of by them, and that they must change about for once, and try to arrange
it in another way. And, though the mouse and the sausage also begged most
earnestly, the bird would have his way, and said it must be tried. They cast
lots about it, and the lot fell on the sausage who was to carry wood, the
mouse became cook, and the bird was to fetch water.

What happened? The little sausage went out towards the wood, the little
bird lighted the fire, the mouse stayed by the pot and waited alone until little
sausage came home and brought wood for next day. But the little sausage
stayed so long on the road that they both feared something was amiss, and
the bird flew out a little way in the air to meet it. Not far off, however, it
met a dog on the road who had fallen on the poor sausage as lawful booty,

The bird sadly took up the wood, flew home, and related what he had seen and heard

and had seized and swallowed it. The bird charged the dog with an act of barefaced robbery, but it was in vain to speak, for the dog said he had found forged letters on the sausage, on which account its life was forfeited to him.

The bird sadly took up the wood, flew home, and related what he had seen and heard. They were much troubled, but agreed to do their best and remain together. The bird therefore laid the cloth, and the mouse made ready the food, and wanted to dress it, and to get into the pot as the sausage used to do, and roll and creep amongst the vegetables to mix them; but before she got into the midst of them she was stopped, and lost her skin and hair and life in the attempt.

When the bird came to carry up the dinner, no cook was there. In its distress the bird threw the wood here and there, called and searched, but no cook was to be found! Owing to his carelessness the wood caught fire, so that a conflagration ensued, the bird hastened to fetch water, and then the bucket dropped from his claws into the well, and he fell down with it, and could not recover himself, but had to drown there.

THE PACK OF RAGAMUFFINS

The cock once said to the hen, "It is now the time when our nuts are ripe, so let us go to the hill together and for once eat our fill before the squirrel takes them all away."

"Yes," replied the hen, "come, we will have some pleasure together."

Then they went away to the hill, and as it was a bright day they stayed till evening.

Now I do not know whether it was that they had eaten till they were too fat, or whether they had become proud, but they would not go home on foot, and the cock had to build a little carriage of nut-shells. When it was ready, the little hen seated herself in it and said to the cock, "Thou canst just harness thyself to it."

"I like that!" said the cock, "I would rather go home on foot than let myself be harnessed to it; no, that is not our bargain. I do not mind being coachman and sitting on the box, but drag it myself I will not."

As they were thus disputing, a duck quacked to them, "You thieving folks, who bade you go to my nut-hill? Wait, you shall suffer for it!" And she ran with open beak at the cock. But the cock also was not idle, and fell boldly on the duck, and at last wounded her so with his spurs that she also begged for mercy, and willingly let herself be harnessed to the carriage as a punishment. The little cock now seated himself on the box and was coachman, and thereupon they went off in a gallop, with "Duck, go as fast as thou canst."

When they had driven a part of the way they met two foot-passengers, a pin and a needle. They cried, "Stop! stop!" and said that it would soon be as dark as pitch, and then they could not go a step further. As it was so dirty on the road, they asked if they could not get into the carriage for a while. They had been at the tailor's public-house by the gate, and had stayed too long over their beer.

As they were thin people, who did not take up much room, the cock let them both get in, but they had to promise him and his little hen not to step on their feet.

Late in the evening they came to an inn, and as they did not like to go further by night, and as the duck also was not strong on her feet, and

*Let us go to the hill together and for once eat our fill before
the squirrel takes them all away*

fell from one side to the other, they went in. The host at first made many objections that his house was already full. Besides, he thought they could not be very distinguished persons. But at last, as they made pleasant speeches, and told him that he should have the egg which the little hen has laid on the way, and should likewise keep the duck, which laid one every day, he at length said that they might stay the night. And now they were well served, and they feasted and rioted.

Early in the morning, when day was breaking, and every one was asleep, the cock awoke the hen. They pecked open the egg, ate it together, and threw the shell on the hearth. Then they went to the needle which was still asleep, took it by the head, and stuck it into the cushion of the landlord's chair. They also put the pin in his towel, and without further ado they flew away over the heath. The duck, who liked to sleep in the open air, had stayed in the yard, and when she heard them going away, she made herself merry and found a stream down which she swam, as this was a much quicker way of travelling than being harnessed to a carriage.

The landlord did not get out of bed until two hours after this. When he went to dry himself after washing, the pin scratched over his face and made a red streak from one ear to the other. After this he went into the kitchen to light a pipe, and saw the eggshell on the hearth.

"This morning everything attacks my head," said he, and angrily sat down on his grandfather's chair. But he quickly started up again and cried, "Woe is me," for the needle had pricked him still worse than the pin, and not in the head.

Now he was thoroughly angry, and suspected the guests who had come so late the night before. And when he looked about for them, he found that they were gone.

Then he made a vow to take no more ragamuffins into his house, for they consume much, pay for nothing, and play mischievous tricks into the bargain by way of gratitude.

CAT AND MOUSE IN PARTNERSHIP

A certain cat had made the acquaintance of a mouse, and had said so much to her about the great love and friendship she felt for her, that at length the mouse agreed that they should live and keep house together.

"But we must make a provision for winter, or else we shall suffer from hunger," said the cat, "and you, little mouse, cannot venture everywhere, or you will be caught in a trap some day."

This good advice was followed, and a pot of fat was bought, but they did not know where to put it. At length, after much consideration, the cat said, "I know no place where it will be better stored up than in the church, for no one dares take anything away from there. We will set it beneath the altar, and not touch it until we are really in need of it."

So the pot was placed in safety, but it was not long before the cat had a great yearning for it, and said to the mouse, "I want to tell you something, little mouse. My cousin has brought a little son into the world, and has asked me to be godmother. He is white with brown spots, and I am to hold him over the font at the christening. Let me go out today, and you look after the house by yourself."

"Yes, yes," answered the mouse, "by all means go, and if you get anything very good, think of me. I should like a drop of sweet red christening wine, too."

All this, however, was untrue; the cat had no cousin, and had not been asked to be godmother. She went straight to the church, stole to the pot of fat, began to lick at it, and licked the top of the fat off. Then she took a walk upon the roofs of the town, looked out for opportunities, and

The cat crept behind the town walls to the church

then stretched herself in the sun, and licked her lips whenever she thought of the pot of fat. Not until it was evening did she return home.

"Well, here you are again," said the mouse, "no doubt you have had a merry day."

"All went off well," answered the cat.

"What name did they give the child?"

"Top off!" said the cat quite coolly.

"Top off!" cried the mouse. "That is a very odd and uncommon name. Is it a usual one in your family?"

"What does it signify?" said the cat. "It is no worse than Crumb-stealer, as your god-children are called."

Before long the cat was seized by another fit of longing. She said to the mouse, "You must do me a favor, and once more manage the house for a day alone. I am again asked to be godmother, and, as the child has a white ring round its neck, I cannot refuse."

The good mouse consented, but the cat crept behind the town walls to the church, and devoured half the pot of fat. "Nothing ever seems so good as what one keeps to oneself," said she, and was quite satisfied with her day's work.

When she went home the mouse inquired, "And what was this child christened?"

"Half-done," answered the cat.

"Half-done! What are you saying? I never heard the name in my life, I'll wager anything it is not in the calendar!"

The cat's mouth soon began to water for some more licking. "All good things go in threes," thought she.

"I am asked to stand godmother again," she told the mouse. "The child is quite black, only it has white paws, but with that exception, it has not a single white hair on its whole body; this only happens once every few years. You will let me go, won't you?"

"Top-off! Half-done!" answered the mouse. "They are such odd names, they make me very thoughtful."

"You sit at home," said the cat, "in your dark-gray fur coat and long tail, and are filled with fancies, that's because you do not go out in the daytime."

During the cat's absence the mouse cleaned the house, and put it in order but the greedy cat entirely emptied the pot of fat. "When everything is eaten up one has some peace," said she to herself, and well filled and fat she did not return home till night.

The mouse at once asked what name had been given to the third child. "It will not please you more than the others," said the cat. "He is named All-gone."

"All-gone," cried the mouse, "that is the most suspicious name of all! I have never seen it in print. All-gone; what can that mean?" and she shook her head, curled herself up, and lay down to sleep.

From this time forth no one invited the cat to be godmother, but when the winter had come and there was no longer anything to be found outside, the mouse thought of their provision, and said, "Come cat, we will go to our pot of fat which we have stored up for ourselves—we shall enjoy that."

"Yes," answered the cat, "you will enjoy it as much as you would enjoy sticking that dainty tongue of yours out of the window."

They set out on their way, but when they arrived, the pot of fat certainly was still in its place, but it was empty. "Alas!" said the mouse, "now I see what has happened, now it comes to light! You are a true friend! You have devoured all when you were standing godmother. First top off, then half done, then—."

"Will you hold your tongue," cried the cat, "one word more and I will eat you too."

"All gone" was already on the poor mouse's lips; scarcely had she spoken it before the cat sprang on her, seized her, and swallowed her down. Verily, that is the way of the world.

※

THE FOX AND THE HORSE

A peasant had a faithful horse which had grown old and could do no more work. So his master would no longer give him anything to eat and said, "I can certainly make no more use of thee, but still I mean well by thee; if thou provest thyself still strong enough to bring me a lion here, I will maintain thee, but now take thyself away out of my stable." And with that he chased him into the open country. The horse was sad, and went to the forest to seek a little protection there from the weather.

Then the fox met him and said, "Why dost thou hang thy head so, and go about all alone?"

"Alas," replied the horse, "avarice and fidelity do not dwell together in one house. My master has forgotten what services I have performed for him for so many years, and because I can no longer plow well, he will give me no more food, and has driven me out."

"Without giving thee a chance?" asked the fox.

"The chance was a bad one. He said, if I were still strong enough to bring him a lion, he would keep me, but he well knows that I cannot do that."

The fox said, "I will help thee. Just lay thyself down, stretch thyself out, as if thou wert dead, and do not stir."

The horse did as the fox desired, and the fox went to the lion, who had his den not far off, and said, "A dead horse is lying outside there. Just come with me, thou canst have a rich meal."

The lion went with him, and when they were both standing by the horse the fox said, "After all, it is not very comfortable for thee here I tell thee what—I will fasten it to thee by the tail, and then thou canst drag it into thy cave, and devour it in peace."

This advice pleased the lion: he lay down, and in order that the fox might tie the horse fast to him, he kept quite quiet. But the fox tied the lion's legs together with the horse's tail, and twisted and fastened all so well and so strongly that no strength could break it. When he had finished his work, he tapped the horse on the shoulder and said, "Pull, white horse, pull."

Then up sprang the horse at once, and drew the lion away with him. The lion began to roar so that all the birds in the forest flew out in terror, but the horse let him roar, and drew him and dragged him over the country to his master's door. When the master saw the lion, he was of a better mind, and said to the horse, "Thou shalt stay with me and fare well," and he gave him plenty to eat until he died.

Then up sprang the horse at once, and drew the lion away with him

THE WOLF AND
THE SEVEN LITTLE KIDS

There was once upon a time an old goat who had seven little kids, and loved them with all the love of a mother for her children. One day she wanted to go into the forest and fetch some food. So she called all seven to her and said, "Dear children, I have to go into the forest, be on your guard against the wolf; if he come in, he will devour you—skin, hair, and all. The wretch often disguises himself, but you will know him at once by his rough voice and his black feet."

The kids said, "Dear mother, we will take good care of ourselves; you may go away without any worry." Then the old one bleated, and went on her way with an easy mind.

It was not long before someone knocked at the house-door and called, "Open the door, dear children; your mother is here, and has brought something back with her for each of you."

But the little kids knew that it was the wolf, by the rough voice; "We will not open the door," cried they, "thou art not our mother. She has a soft, pleasant voice, but thy voice is rough; thou art the wolf!"

Then the wolf went away to a shopkeeper and bought himself a great lump of chalk, ate this and made his voice soft with it. The he came back, knocked at the door of the house, and cried, "Open the door, dear children, your mother is here and has brought something back with her for each of you."

But the wolf had laid his black paws against the window, and the children saw them and cried, "We will not open the door, our mother has not black feet like thee: thou art the wolf!"

Then the wolf ran to a baker and said, "I have hurt my feet, rub some dough over them for me."

And when the baker had rubbed his feet over, he ran to the miller and said, "Strew some white meal over my feet for me."

The miller thought to himself, "The wolf wants to deceive some one," and refused; but the wolf said, "If thou wilt not do it, I will devour thee." Then the miller was afraid, and made his paws white for him. Truly men are like that.

So now the wretch went for the third time to the house of the goat, knocked at it, and said, "Open the door for me, children, your dear little mother has come home, and has brought every one of you something back from the forest with her."

The little kids cried, "First show us thy paws that we may know if thou art our dear little mother."

Then he put his paws in through the window, and when the kids saw that they were white, they believed that all he said was true, and opened the door. But who should come in but the wolf!

They were terrified and wanted to hide themselves. One sprang under the table, the second into the bed, the third into the stove, the fourth into the kitchen, the fifth into the cupboard, the sixth under the washing-bowl, and the seventh into the clock-case. But the wolf found them all, and used no great ceremony; one after the other he swallowed them down his throat. The youngest, who was in the clock-case, was the only one he did not find.

When the wolf had satisfied his appetite he took himself off, laid himself down under a tree in the green meadow outside, and began to sleep.

Soon afterwards the old goat came home again from the forest. Ah! what a sight she saw there! The house-door stood wide open. The table, chairs, and benches were thrown down, the washing-bowl lay broken to pieces, and the quilts and pillows were pulled off the bed. She sought her children, but they were nowhere to be found. She called them one after another by name, but no one answered. At last, when she came to the youngest, a soft voice cried, "Dear mother, I am in the clock-case." She took the kid out, and it told her that the wolf had come and had eaten all the others. Then you may imagine how she wept over her poor children.

At length in her grief she went out, and the youngest kid ran with her. When they came to the meadow, there lay the wolf by the tree and snored so loud that the branches shook. She looked at him on every side and saw that something was moving and struggling in his gorged belly. "Ah, heavens," said she, "is it possible that my poor children whom he has swallowed down for his supper, can be still alive?"

Then the kid had to run home and fetch scissors, and a needle and thread, and the goat cut open the monster's stomach, and hardly had she make one cut, than one little kid thrust its head out, and when she cut farther, all six sprang out one after another, and were all still alive, and had suffered no injury whatever, for in his greediness the monster had swallowed

. . . and danced for joy round about the well with their mother

them down whole. What rejoicing there was! They embraced their dear mother, and jumped like a tailor at his wedding.

The mother, however, said, "Now go and look for some big stones, and we will fill the wicked beast's stomach with them while he is still asleep." Then the seven kids dragged the stones thither with all speed, and put as many of them into his stomach as they could get in; and the mother sewed him up again in the greatest haste, so that he was not aware of anything and never once stirred.

When the wolf at length had had his sleep out, he got on his legs, and as the stones in his stomach made him very thirsty, he wanted to go to a well to drink. But when he began to walk and move about, the stones in his stomach knocked against each other and rattled. Then cried he,

> What rumbles and tumbles
> Against my poor bones?
> I thought 'twas six kids,
> But it's naught but big stones.

And when he got to the well and stooped over the water and was just about to drink, the heavy stones made him fall in, and there was no help, but he had to drown miserably. When the seven kids saw that, they came running to the spot and cried aloud, "The wolf is dead! The wolf is dead!" and danced for joy round about the well with their mother.

LITTLE RED RIDING HOOD

Once upon a time there was a dear little girl who was loved by every one who looked at her, but most of all by her grandmother; and there was nothing that she would not have given to the child. Once she gave her a little cap of red velvet, which suited her so well that she would never wear anything else; so she was always called "Little Red Riding Hood."

One day her mother said to her, "Come, Little Red Riding Hood, here is a piece of cake and a bottle of wine; take them to your grandmother. She is ill and weak, and they will do her good. Set out before it gets hot, and when you

And just as Little Red Riding Hood entered the wood, a wolf met her

are going, walk nicely and quietly and do not run off the path, or you may fall and break the bottle, and then your grandmother will get nothing. And when you go into her room, don't forget to say, 'Good-morning,' and don't peep into every corner before you do it."

"I will take great care," said Little Red Riding Hood to her mother, and gave her hand on it.

The grandmother lived out in the wood, half a league from the village, and just as Little Red Riding Hood entered the wood, a wolf met her. Red Riding Hood did not know what a wicked creature he was, and was not at all afraid of him.

"Good-day, Little Red Riding Hood," said he.

"Thank you kindly, wolf."

"Whither away so early, Little Red Riding Hood?"

"To my grandmother's."

"What have you got in your apron?"

"Cake and wine; yesterday was baking-day, so poor sick grandmother is to have something good, to make her stronger."

"Where does your grandmother live, Little Red Riding Hood?"

"A good quarter of a league farther on in the wood; her house stands under the three large oak-trees, the nut-trees are just below; you surely must know it," replied Little Red Riding Hood.

The wolf thought to himself, "What a tender young creature! what a nice plump mouthful—she will be better to eat than the old woman. I must act craftily, so as to catch both." So he walked for a short time by the side of Little Red Riding Hood, and then he said, "See Little Red Riding Hood, how pretty the flowers are about here—why do you not look round? I believe, too, that you do not hear how sweetly the little birds are singing; you walk gravely along as if you were going to school, while everything else out here in the wood is merry."

Little Red Riding Hood raised her eyes, and when she saw the sun-beams dancing here and there through the trees, and pretty flowers growing everywhere, she thought, "Suppose I take grandmother a fresh nosegay; that would please her too. It is so early in the day that I shall still get there in good time"; and so she ran from the path into the wood to look for flowers. And when she had picked one, she fancied that she saw a still prettier one farther on, and ran after it, and so got deeper and deeper into the wood.

Meanwhile the wolf ran straight to the grandmother's house and knocked at the door.

"Who is there?"

"Little Red Riding Hood," replied the wolf. "I have brought cake and wine; open the door."

"Lift the latch," called out the grandmother. "I am too weak, and cannot get up."

The wolf lifted the latch, the door flew open, and without saying a word he went straight to the grandmother's bed, and devoured her. Then he put on her clothes, dressed himself in her cap, laid himself in bed and drew the curtains.

Little Red Riding Hood, however, had been running about picking flowers, and when she had gathered so many that she could carry no more, she remembered her grandmother, and set out on the way to her.

She was surprised to find the cottage-door standing open, and when she went into the room, she had such a strange feeling that she said to herself, "Oh dear! how uneasy I feel today, whereas at other times I like being with grandmother so much." She called out, "Good morning," but received no answer; so she went to the bed and drew back the curtains. There lay her grandmother with her cap pulled far over her face, and looking very strange.

"Oh! grandmother," she said, "what big ears you have!"

"The better to hear you with, my child," was the reply.

"But, grandmother, what big eyes you have!" she said.

"The better to see you with, my dear."

"But, grandmother, what large hands you have!"

"The better to hug you with."

"Oh! but, grandmother, what a terrible big mouth you have!"

"The better to eat you with!"

And scarcely had the wolf said this, than with one bound he was out of bed and swallowed up Red Riding Hood.

When the wolf had appeased his appetite, he lay down again in the bed, fell asleep and began to snore very loud.

The huntsman was just passing the house, and thought to himself, "How the old woman is snoring! I must just see if she wants anything."

"Oh! grandmother," she said, "what big ears you have!"

So he went into the room, and when he came to the bed, he saw that the wolf was lying in it. "Do I find thee here, thou old sinner!" said he. "I have long sought thee!"

Then just as he was going to fire at him, it occurred to him that the wolf might have devoured the grandmother, and that she might still be saved, so he did not fire, but took a pair of scissors, and began to cut open the stomach of the sleeping wolf. When he had made two snips, he saw the little red riding hood shining, and then he made two snips more, and the little girl sprang out, crying, "Ah, how frightened I have been! How dark it was inside the wolf. And after that the aged grandmother came out alive also, but scarcely able to breathe. Red Riding Hood, however, quickly fetched great stones with which they filled the wolf's body, and when he awoke, he wanted to run away, but the stones were so heavy that he fell down at once, and fell dead.

Then all three were delighted. The huntsman drew off the wolf's skin and went home with it; the grandmother ate the cake and drank the wine which Red Riding Hood had brought, and revived, but Red Riding Hood thought to herself, "As long as I live, I will never by myself leave the path, to run into the wood, when my mother has forbidden me to do so."

It is also related that once when Red Riding Hood was again taking cakes to the old grandmother, another wolf spoke to her, and tried to entice her from the path. Red Riding Hood, however, was on her guard, and went straight forward on her way, and told her grandmother that she had met the wolf, and that he had said "good-morning" to her, but with such a wicked look in his eyes, that if they had not been on the public road she was certain he would have eaten her up.

"Well," said the grandmother, "we will shut the door, that he may not come in."

Soon afterwards the wolf knocked, and cried, "Open the door, grandmother, I am little Red Riding Hood, and am fetching you some cakes." But they did not speak, or open the door, so the graybeard stole twice or thrice round the house, and at last jumped on the roof, intending to wait until Red Riding Hood went home in the evening, and then to steal after her and devour her in the darkness.

But the grandmother saw what was in his thoughts. In front of the house was a great stone trough, so she said to the child, "Take the pail,

Red Riding Hood; I made some sausages yesterday, so carry the water in which I boiled them to the trough."

Red Riding Hood carried until the great trough was quite full. Then the smell of the sausages reached the wolf, and he sniffed and peeped down, and at last stretched out his neck so far that he could no longer keep his footing and began to slip, and slipped down from the roof straight into the great trough, and was drowned. Then Red Riding Hood went joyously home, and never did anything to harm anyone.

THE FOUNDLING BIRD

There was once a forester who went into the forest to hunt, and as he entered it he heard a sound of screaming as if a little child were there. He followed the sound, and at last came to a high tree. At the top of this a little child was sitting, for the mother had fallen asleep under the tree with the child, and a bird of prey had seen it in her arms, had flown down, snatched it away, and set it on the high tree.

The forester climbed up, brought the child down, and thought to himself, "Thou wilt take him home with thee, and bring him up with thy Lina."

He took it home, therefore, and the two children grew up together. The one, however, which he had found on a tree was called a foundling bird, because a bird had carried it away. The foundling and Lina loved each other so dearly that when they did not see each other they were sad.

The forester, however, had an old cook, who one evening took two pails and began to fetch water, and did not go once only, but many times, out to the spring.

Lina saw this and said, "Hark you, old Sanna, why are you fetching so much water?"

"If thou wilt never repeat it to anyone, I will tell thee why."

So Lina said, no, she would never repeat it to anyone, and then the cook said, "Early tomorrow morning, when the forester is out hunting, I will heat the water, and when it is boiling in the kettle, I will throw in the foundling, and will boil him in it."

*The forester, however, had an old cook, who one evening took two pails
and began to fetch water*

Betimes next morning the forester got up and went out hunting, and when he was gone the children were still in bed. Then Lina said to the foundling, "If thou wilt never leave me, I too will never leave thee."

The foundling said, "Neither now, nor ever will I leave thee."

Then said Lina, "Then I will tell thee. Last night, old Sanna carried so many buckets of water into the house that I asked her why she was doing that, and she said that if I would promise not to tell any one she would tell me, and I said I would be sure not to tell any one, and she said that early tomorrow morning when father was out hunting, she would set the kettle full of water, throw thee into it and boil thee; but we will get up quickly, dress ourselves, and go away together."

The two children therefore got up, dressed themselves quickly, and went away. When the water in the kettle was boiling, the cook went into the bedroom to fetch the foundling and throw him into it. But when she came in, and went to the beds, both the children were gone. Then she was terribly alarmed, and she said to herself, "What shall I say now when the forester comes home and sees that the children are gone? They must be followed instantly to get them back again."

Then the cook sent three servants after them, who were to run and overtake the children. The children, however, were sitting outside the forest, and when they saw from afar the three servants running, Lina said to the foundling, "Never leave me, and I will never leave thee."

The foundling said, "Neither now, nor ever."

Then said Lina, "Do thou become a rose-tree, and I the rose upon it."

When the three servants came to the forest, nothing was there but a rose-tree and one rose on it, but the children were nowhere. Then said they, "There is nothing to be done here," and they went home and told the cook that they had seen nothing in the forest but a little rose-bush with one rose on it.

Then the old cook scolded and said, "You simpletons, you should have cut the rose-bush in two, and have broken off the rose and brought it home with you; go, and do it once." They had therefore to go out and look for the second time.

The children, however, saw them coming from a distance.

Then Lina said, "Foundling bird, never leave me, and I will never leave thee."

The foundling said, "Neither now, nor ever."

Said Lina, "Then do thou become a church, and I'll be the chandelier in it."

So when the three servants came, nothing was there but a church, with a chandelier in it. They said therefore to each other, "What can we do here, let us go home." When they got home, the cook asked if they had not found them; so they said no, they had found nothing but a church, and that there was a chandelier in it.

And the cook scolded them and said, "You fools! why did you not pull the church to pieces, and bring the chandelier home with you?"

And now the old cook herself got on her legs, and went with the three servants in pursuit of the children.

The children, however, saw from afar that the three servants were coming, and the cook waddling after them.

Then said Lina, "Foundling bird, never leave me, and I will never leave thee."

Then said the foundling, "Neither now, nor ever."

Said Lina, "Be a fishpond, and I will be the duck upon it."

The cook, however, came up to them, and when she saw the pond she lay down by it, and was about to drink it up. But the duck swam quickly to her, seized her head in its beak and drew her into the water, and there the old witch had to drown.

Then the children went home together, and were heartily delighted, and if they are not dead, they are living still.

❧

THE WILLOW-WREN AND THE BEAR

Once in summer-time the bear and the wolf were walking in the forest, and the bear heard a bird singing so beautifully that he said, "Brother wolf, what bird is it that sings so well?"

"That is the King of birds," said the wolf, "before whom we must bow down."

It was, however, in reality the willow-wren.

"If that's the case," said the bear, "I should very much like to see his royal palace; come, take me thither."

"That is not done quite as you seem to think," said the wolf; "you must wait until the Queen comes."

Soon afterwards, the Queen arrived with some food in her beak, and the lord King came too, and they began to feed their young ones. The bear would have liked to go at once, but the wolf held him back by the sleeve, and said, "No, you must wait until the lord and lady Queen have gone away again." So they observed the hole in which was the nest, and trotted away.

The bear, however, could not rest until he had seen the royal palace, and when a short time had passed, again went to it. The King and Queen had just flown out, so he peeped in and saw five or six young ones lying in it. "Is that the royal palace?" cried the bear; "it is a wretched palace, and you are not King's children, you are disreputable children!"

When the young wrens heard that, they were frightfully angry, and screamed, "No, that we are not! Our parents are honest people! Bear, thou wilt have to pay for that!"

The bear and the wolf grew uneasy, and turned back and went into their holes. The young willow-wrens, however, continued to cry and scream, and when their parents again brought food they said, "We will not so much as touch one fly's leg, no, not if we were dying of hunger, until you have settled whether we are respectable children or not; the bear has been here and has insulted us!"

Then the old King said, "Be easy, he shall be punished," and he at once flew with the Queen to the bear's cave, and called in, "Old Growler, why hast thou insulted my children? Thou shalt suffer for it we will punish thee by a bloody war."

Thus war was announced to the Bear, and all four-footed animals were summoned to take part in it—oxen, asses, cows, deer, and every other animal the earth contained. And the willow-wren summoned everything which flew in the air—not only birds, large and small, but midges, and hornets, bees and flies had to come.

When the time came for the war to begin, the willow-wren sent out spies to discover who was the enemy's commander-in-chief. The gnat, who was the most crafty, flew into the forest where the enemy was assembled, and hid herself beneath a leaf of the tree where the watchword was to be given.

There stood the bear, and he called the fox before him and said, "Fox, thou art the most cunning of all animals, thou shalt be general and lead us."

"Good," said the fox, "but what signal shall we agree upon?" No one knew that, so the fox said, "I have a fine long bushy tail, which almost looks like a plume of red feathers. When I lift my tail up quite high, all is going well, and you must charge; but if I let it hang down, run away as fast as you can." When the gnat had heard that, she flew away again, and revealed everything, with the greatest minuteness, to the willow-wren.

When day broke, and the battle was to begin, all the four-footed animals came running up with such a noise that the earth trembled. The willow-wren also came flying through the air with his army with such a humming, and whirring, and swarming that every one was uneasy and afraid, and on both sides they advanced against each other. But the willow-wren sent down the hornet, with orders to get beneath the fox's tail, and sting with all his might. When the fox felt the first sting, he started so that he drew up one leg, with the pain, but he bore it, and still kept his tail high in the air; at the second sting, he was forced to put it down for a moment; at the third, he could hold out no longer, and screamed out and put his tail between his legs. When the animals saw that, they thought all was lost, and began to fly, each into his hole and the birds had won the battle.

Then the King and Queen flew home to their children and cried, "Children, rejoice, eat and drink to your heart's content, we have won the battle!"

But the young wrens said, "We will not eat yet, the bear must come to the nest, and beg for pardon and say that we are honorable children, before we will do that."

Then the willow-wren flew to the bear's hole and cried, "Growler, thou art to come to the nest to my children, and beg their pardon, or else every rib of thy body shall be broken."

So the bear crept thither in the greatest fear, and begged their pardon. And now at last the young wrens were satisfied, and sat down together and ate and drank, and made merry till quite late into the night.

At the third, he could hold out no longer, and screamed out and put his tail between his legs

SWEETHEART ROLAND

There was once on a time a woman who was a real witch and had two daughters, one ugly and wicked, and this one she loved because she was her own daughter, and one beautiful and good, and this one she hated, because she was her stepdaughter. The stepdaughter once had a pretty apron, which the other fancied so much that she became envious, and told her mother that she must and would have that apron.

"Be quiet, my child," said the old woman, "and thou shalt have it. Thy stepsister has long deserved death, tonight when she is asleep I will come and cut her head off. Only be careful that thou art at the far-side of the bed, and push her well to the front."

It would have been all over with the poor girl if she had not just then been standing in a corner, and heard everything. All day long she dared not go out of doors, and when bed-time had come, the witch's daughter got into bed first, so as to lie at the far-side, but when she was asleep, the other pushed her gently to the front, and took for herself the place at the back, close by the wall. In the night, the old woman came creeping in, she held an ax in her right hand, and felt with her left to see if anyone was lying at the outside, and then she grasped the ax with both hands, and cut her own child's head off.

When she had gone away, the girl got up and went to her sweetheart, who was called Roland, and knocked at his door. When he came out, she said to him, "Hear me, dearest Roland, we must fly in all haste; my stepmother wanted to kill me, but has struck her own child. When daylight comes, and she sees what she has done, we shall be lost."

"But," said Roland, "I counsel thee first to take away her magic wand, or we cannot escape if she pursues us." The maiden fetched the magic wand, and she took the dead girl's head and dropped three drops of blood on the ground, one in front of the bed, one in the kitchen, and one on the stairs. Then she hurried away with her lover.

When the old witch got up next morning, she called her daughter, and wanted to give her the apron, but she did not come. Then the witch cried, "Where art thou?"

"Here, on the stairs, I am sweeping," answered the first drop of blood.

The maiden fetched the magic wand, and she took the dead girl's head and dropped three drops of blood on the ground

The old woman went out, but saw no one on the stairs, and cried again, "Where art thou?"

"Here in the kitchen, I am warming myself," cried the second drop of blood.

She went into the kitchen, but found no one. Then she cried again, "Where art thou?"

"Ah, here in the bed, I am sleeping," cried the third drop of blood.

She went into the room to the bed. What did she see there? Her own child, whose head she had cut off, bathed in her blood. The witch fell into a passion, sprang to the window, and as she could look forth quite far into the world, she perceived her stepdaughter hurrying away with her sweetheart Roland.

"That shall not serve you," cried she, "even if you have got a long way off, you shall still not escape me." She put on her many league boots, in which went an hour's walk at every step, and it was not long before she overtook them. The girl, however, when she saw the old woman striding towards her, changed, with her magic wand, her sweetheart Roland into a lake, and herself into a duck swimming in the middle of it. The witch placed herself on the shore, threw bread-crumbs in, and gave herself every possible trouble to entice the duck; but the duck did not let herself be enticed, and the old woman had to go home at night as she had come.

On this the girl and her sweetheart Roland resumed their natural shapes again, and they walked on the whole night until daybreak. Then the maiden changed herself into a beautiful flower which stood in the midst of a briar hedge, and her sweetheart Roland into a fiddler. It was not long before the witch came striding up towards them, and said to the musician, "Dear musician, may I pluck that beautiful flower for myself?" "Oh, yes," he replied, "I will play to you while you do it."

As she was hastily creeping into the hedge and was just going to pluck the flower, for she well knew who the flower was, he began to play, and whether she would or not, she was forced to dance, for it was a magical dance. The quicker he played, the more violent springs was she forced to make, and the thorns tore her clothes from her body, and pricked her and wounded her till she bled, and as he did not stop, she had to dance till she lay dead on the ground.

When they were delivered, Roland said, "Now I will go to my father and arrange for the wedding."

The quicker he played, the more violent springs was she forced to make

"Then in the meantime I will stay here and wait for thee," said the girl, "and that no one may recognize me, I will change myself into a red stone land-mark."

Then Roland went away, and the girl stood like a red land-mark in the field and waited for her beloved. But when Roland got home, he fell into the snares of another, who prevailed on him so far that he forgot the maiden. The poor girl remained there a long time, but at length, as he did not return at all, she was sad, and changed herself into a flower, and thought, "Someone will surely come this way, and trample me down."

It befell, however, that a shepherd kept his sheep in the field, and saw the flower, and as it was so pretty, plucked it, took it with him, and laid it away in his chest. From that time forth, strange things happened in the shepherd's house. When he arose in the morning, all the work was already done, the room was swept, the table and benches cleaned, the fire on the hearth was lighted, and the water was fetched, and at noon, when he came home, the table was laid, and a good dinner served. He could not conceive how this came to pass, for he never saw a human being in his house, and no one could have concealed himself in it. He was certainly pleased with this good attendance, but still at last he was so afraid that he went to a wise woman and asked for her advice. The wise woman said, "There is some enchantment behind it, listen very early some morning if anything is moving in the room, and if thou seest anything, let it be what it may, throw a white cloth over it, and then the magic will be stopped."

The shepherd did as she bade him, and next morning just as day dawned, he saw the chest open, and the flower come out. Swiftly he sprang towards it, and threw a white cloth over it. Instantly the transformation came to an end, and a beautiful girl stood before him, who owned to him that she had been the flower, and that up to this time she had attended to his housekeeping. She told him her story, and as she pleased him he asked her if she would marry him, but she answered, "No," for she wanted to remain faithful to her sweetheart Roland, although he had deserted her, but she promised not to go away, but to keep house for the shepherd for the future.

And now the time drew near when Roland's wedding was to be celebrated, and then, according to an old custom in the country, it was announced that all the girls were to be present at it, and sing in honor of the bridal pair. When the faithful maiden heard of this, she grew so sad that she thought her heart would break, and she would not go thither, but the other girls came and took her. When it came to her turn to sing, she stepped back, until at last she was the only one left, and then she could not refuse. But when she began her song, and it reached Roland's ears, he sprang up and cried, "I know the voice, that is the true bride, I will have no other!" Everything he had forgotten, and which had vanished from his mind, had suddenly come home again to his heart. Then the faithful maiden held her wedding with her sweetheart Roland, and grief came to an end and joy began.

⤫

MOTHER HOLLE

There was once a widow who had two daughters—one of whom was pretty and industrious, whilst the other was ugly and idle. But she was much fonder of the ugly and idle one, because she was her own daughter; and the other, who was a stepdaughter, was obliged to do all the work, and be the Cinderella of the house. Every day the poor girl had to sit by a well, in the highway, and spin and spin till her fingers bled.

Now it happened that one day the shuttle was marked with her blood, so she dipped it in the well to wash the mark off; but it dropped out of her hand and fell to the bottom. She began to weep, and ran to her stepmother and told her of the mishap. But her stepmother scolded her sharply, and was so merciless as to say, "Since you have let the shuttle fall in, you must fetch it out again."

So the girl went back to the well, and did not know what to do; and in the sorrow of her heart she jumped into the well to get the shuttle. She lost her senses; and when she awoke and came to herself again, she was in a lovely meadow where the sun was shining and many thousands of flowers were growing. Along this meadow she went, and at last came to a baker's oven full of bread, and the bread cried out, "Oh, take me out! take me out! or I shall burn; I have been baked a long time!"

So she went up to it, and took out all the loaves one after another with the bread-shovel. After that she went on till she came to a tree covered with apples, which called out to her, "Oh, shake me! shake me! we apples are all ripe!" So she shook the tree till the apples fell like rain, and went on shaking

At last she came to a little house, out of which an old woman peeped

till they were all down, and when she had gathered them into a heap, she went
on her way.

At last she came to a little house, out of which an old woman peeped; but
she had such large teeth that the girl was frightened, and was about to run away.

But the old woman called out to her, "What are you afraid of, dear child?
Stay with me; if you will do all the work in the house properly, you shall be
the better for it. Only you must take care to make my bed well, and shake
it thoroughly till the feathers fly—for then there is snow on the earth. I am
Mother Holle.

As the old woman spoke so kindly to her, the girl took courage and
agreed to enter her service. She attended to everything to the satisfaction of
her mistress, and always shook her bed so vigorously that the feathers flew
about like snow-flakes. So she had a pleasant life with her; never an angry
word; and she was given boiled or roast meat every day.

She stayed some time with Mother Holle, and then she became sad.
At first she did not know what was the matter with her, but found at length
that it was home-sickness: although she was many thousand times better

off here than at home, still she had a longing to be there. At last she said to the old woman, "I have a longing for home; and however well off I am down here, I cannot stay any longer; I must go up again to my own people."

Mother Holle said, "I am pleased that you long for your home again, and as you have served me so truly, I myself will take you up again." Thereupon she took her by the hand, and led her to a large door.

The door was opened, and just as the maiden was standing beneath the doorway, a heavy shower of golden rain fell, and all the gold remained sticking to her, so that she was completely covered over with it.

"You shall have that because you have been so industrious," said Mother Holle, and at the same time she gave her back the shuttle which she had let fall into the well. Thereupon the door closed, and the maiden found herself up above upon the earth, not far from her mother's house.

And as she went into the yard the cock was standing by the well-side, and cried—

Cock-a-doodle-doo!
Your golden girl's come back to you!

So she went in to her mother, and as she arrived thus covered with gold, she was well received, both by her and her sister.

The girl told all that had happened to her; and as soon as the mother heard how she had come by so much wealth, she was very anxious to obtain the same good luck for the ugly and lazy daughter. She had to seat herself by the well and spin; and in order that her shuttle might be stained with blood, she stuck her hand into a thorn bush and pricked her finger. Then she threw her shuttle into the well, and jumped in after it.

She came, like the other, to the beautiful meadow and walked along the very same path. When she got to the oven the bread again cried, "Oh, take me out! take me out! or I shall burn; I have been baked a long time!" But the lazy thing answered, "As if I had any wish to make myself dirty?" and on she went. Soon she came to the apple-tree, which cried, "Oh, shake me! shake me! we apples are all ripe!" But she answered, "I like that! one of you might fall on my head," and so went on.

When she came to Mother Holle's house she was not afraid, for she had already heard of her big teeth, and she hired herself to her immediately.

But the pitch stuck fast to her, and could not be got off as long as she lived

The first day she forced herself to work diligently, and obeyed Mother Holle when she told her to do anything, for she was thinking of all the gold that she would give her. But on the second day she began to be lazy, and on the third day still more so, and then she would not get up in the morning at all. Neither did she make Mother Holle's bed as she ought, and did not shake it so as to make the feathers fly up. Mother Holle was soon tired of this, and gave her notice to leave. The lazy girl was willing enough to go, and thought that now the golden rain would come. Mother Holle led her also to the great door; but while she was standing beneath it, instead of the gold a big kettleful of pitch was emptied over her. "That is the reward for your service," said Mother Holle, and shut the door.

So the lazy girl went home; but she was quite covered with pitch, and the cock by the well-side, as soon as he saw her, cried out—

> Cock-a-doodle-doo!
> Your pitchy girl's come back to you!

But the pitch stuck fast to her, and could not be got off as long as she lived.

THE WHITE SNAKE

A long time ago there lived a king who was famed for his wisdom through all the land. Nothing was hidden from him, and it seemed as if news of the most secret things was brought to him through the air. But he had a strange custom; every day after dinner, when the table was cleared, and no one else was present, a trusty servant had to bring him one more dish. It was covered, however, and even the servant did not know what was in it, neither did anyone know, for the King never took off the cover to eat of it until he was quite alone.

This had gone on for a long time, when one day the servant, who took away the dish, was overcome with such curiosity that he could not help carrying the dish into his room. When he had carefully locked the door, he lifted up the cover, and saw a white snake lying on the dish. But when he saw it he could not deny himself the pleasure of tasting it, so he cut off a little bit and put it into his mouth. No sooner had it touched his tongue than he heard a strange whispering of little voices outside his window. He went and listened, and then noticed that it was the sparrows who were chattering together, and telling one another of all kinds of things which they had seen in the fields and woods. Eating the snake had given him power of understanding the language of animals.

Now it so happened that on this very day the Queen lost her most beautiful ring, and suspicion of having stolen it fell upon this trusty servant, who was allowed to go everywhere. The King ordered the man to be brought before him, and threatened with angry words that unless he could before the morrow point out the thief, he himself should be looked upon as guilty and executed. In vain he declared his innocence; he was dismissed with no better answer.

In his trouble and fear he went down into the courtyard and took thought how to help himself out of his trouble. Now some ducks were sitting together quietly by a brook and taking their rest; and, whilst they were making their feathers smooth with their bills, they were having a confidential conversation together. The servant stood by and listened. They were telling one another of all the places where they had been waddling about all the morning, and what good food they had found, and one said in a pitiful tone, "Something lies

They quivered with delight, put out their heads, and cried to him,
"We will remember you and repay you for saving us!"

heavy on my stomach; as I was eating in haste I swallowed a ring which lay under the Queen's window."

The servant at once seized her by the neck, carried her to the kitchen, and said to the cook, "Here is a fine duck; pray, kill her."

"Yes," said the cook, and weighed her in his hand; "she has spared no trouble to fatten herself, and has been waiting to be roasted long enough." So he cut off her head, and as she was being dressed for the spit, the Queen's ring was found inside her.

The servant could now easily prove his innocence; and the King, to make amends for the wrong, allowed him to ask a favor, and promised him the best place in the court that he could wish for. The servant refused everything, and only asked for a horse and some money for traveling, as he had a mind to see the world and go about a little.

When his request was granted he set out on his way, and one day came to a pond, where he saw three fishes caught in the reeds and gasping for water. Now, though it is said that fishes are dumb, he heard them lamenting that they must perish so miserably, and, as he had a kind heart, he got off his horse and put the three prisoners back into the water. They quivered with delight, put out their heads, and cried to him, "We will remember you and repay you for saving us!"

He rode on, and after a while it seemed to him that he heard a voice in the sand at his feet. He listened, and heard an ant-king complain, "Why cannot folks, with their clumsy beasts, keep off our bodies? That stupid horse, with his heavy hoofs, has been treading down my people without mercy!"

So he turned on to a side path and the ant-king cried out to him, "We will remember you—one good turn deserves another!"

The path led him into a wood, and here he saw two old ravens standing by their nest, and throwing out their young ones.

"Out with you, you idle, good-for-nothing creatures!" cried they; "we cannot find food for you any longer; you are big enough, and can provide for yourselves." But the poor young ravens lay upon the ground, flapping their wings, and crying, "Oh, what helpless chicks we are! We must shift for ourselves, and yet we cannot fly! What can we do, but lie here and starve?"

So the good young fellow alighted and killed his horse with his sword, and gave it to them for food. Then they came hopping up to it, satisfied their hunger, and cried, "We will remember you—one good turn deserves another!"

And now he had to use his own legs, and when he had walked a long way, he came to a large city. There was a great noise and crowd in the streets, and a man rode up on horseback, crying aloud, "The King's daughter wants a husband; but whoever sues for her hand must perform a hard task, and if he does not succeed he will forfeit his life."

Many had already made the attempt, but in vain; nevertheless when the youth saw the King's daughter he was so overcome by her great beauty that he forgot all danger, went before the King, and declared himself a suitor.

So he was led out to the sea, and a gold ring was thrown into it, in his sight; then the King ordered him to fetch this ring up from the bottom of the sea, and added, "If you come up again without it you will be thrown in again and again until you perish amid the waves."

All the people grieved for the handsome youth; then they went away, leaving him alone by the sea. He stood on the shore and considered what he should do, when suddenly he saw three fishes come swimming towards him, and they were the very fishes whose lives he had saved. The one in the middle held a mussel in its mouth, which it laid on the shore at the youth's feet, and when he had taken it up and opened it, there lay the gold ring in the shell. Full of joy he took it to the King, and expected that he would grant him the promised reward. But when the proud princess perceived that he was not her equal in birth, she scorned him, and required him first to perform another task. She went down into the garden and strewed with her own hands ten sacks-full of millet-seed on the grass; then she said, "Tomorrow morning before sunrise these must be picked up, and not a single grain be wanting."

The youth sat down in the garden and considered how it might be possible to perform this task, but he could think of nothing, and there he sat sorrowfully awaiting the break of day, when he should be led to death. But as soon as the first rays of the sun shone into the garden he saw all the ten sacks standing side by side, quite full, and not a single grain was missing. The ant-king had come in the night with thousands and thousands of ants, and the grateful creatures had by great industry picked up all the millet-seed and gathered them into the sacks.

Presently the King's daughter herself came down into the garden, and was amazed to see that the young man had done the task she had given him.

But she could not yet conquer her proud heart, and said, "Although he has performed both the tasks, he shall not be my husband until he has brought me an apple from the Tree of Life."

The youth did not know where the Tree of Life stood, but he set out, and would have gone on for ever, as long as his legs would carry him, though he had no hope of finding it. After he had wandered through three kingdoms, he came one evening to a wood, and lay down under a tree to sleep. But he heard a rustling in the branches, and a golden apple fell into his hand. At the same time three ravens flew down to him, perched themselves upon his knee, and said, "We are the three young ravens whom you saved from starving; when we had grown big, and heard that you were seeking the Golden Apple, we flew over the sea to the end of the world, where the Tree of Life stands, and have brought you the apple."

The youth, full of joy, set out homewards, and took the Golden Apple to the King's beautiful daughter, who had no more excuses left to make.

They cut the Apple of Life in two and ate it together; and then her heart became full of love for him, and they lived in undisturbed happiness to a great age.

❦

THE QUEEN BEE

Two kings' sons once went out in search of adventures, and fell into a wild, disorderly way of living, so that they never came home again. The youngest, who was called Simpleton, set out to seek his brothers, but when at length he found them they mocked him for thinking that he, with his simplicity, could get through the world, when they two could not make their way, and yet were so much cleverer. They all three traveled away together, and came to an ant-hill. The two elder wanted to destroy it, to see the little ants creeping about in their terror, and carrying their eggs away, but Simpleton said, "Leave the creatures in peace; I will not allow you to disturb them."

Then they went onwards and came to a lake, on which a great number of ducks were swimming. The two brothers wanted to catch a couple and roast them, but Simpleton would not permit it, and said, "Leave the creatures in peace; I will not suffer you to kill them."

At length they came to a bee's nest, in which there was so much honey that it ran out of the trunk of the tree where it was. The two wanted to make a fire beneath the tree, and suffocate the bees in order to take away the honey, but Simpleton again stopped them and said, "Leave the creatures in peace; I will not allow you to burn them."

At length the three brothers arrived at a castle where stone horses were standing in the stables, and no human being was to be seen. They went through all the halls until, quite at the end, they came to a door in which were three locks. In the middle of the door, however, there was a little pane, through which they could see into the room. There they saw a little gray man, who was sitting at a table. They called him, once, twice, but he did not hear; at last they called him for the third time, whereupon he got up, opened the locks, and came out. He said nothing, however, but conducted them to a handsomely-spread table, and when they had eaten and drunk, he took each of them to a bedroom.

Next morning the little gray man came to the eldest, beckoned to him, and conducted him to a stone table, on which were inscribed three tasks, by the performance of which the castle could be delivered. The first was that in the forest, beneath the moss, lay the princess's pearls, a thousand in number, which must be picked up; and if by sunset one single pearl was wanting, he who had looked for them would be turned into stone. The eldest went thither, and sought the whole day; but when it came to an end, he had only found one hundred, and what was written on the table came to pass, and he was changed into stone. Next day, the second brother undertook the adventure; it did not, however, fare much better with him than with the eldest; he did not find more than two hundred pearls, and was changed to stone.

At last the turn came to Simpleton also, who sought in the moss. It was, however, so hard to find the pearls, and he got on so slowly, that he seated himself on a stone and wept. And while he was thus sitting, the King of the ants whose life he had once saved, came with five thousand ants, and before long the little creatures had got all the pearls together, and laid them in a heap.

The second task was to fetch out of the lake the key of the King's daughter's bedchamber. When Simpleton came to the lake, the ducks which he had saved swam up to him, dived down, and brought the key out of the water.

The ducks which he had saved swam up to him, dived
down, and brought the key out of the water

The third task was the most difficult: from among the three sleeping daughters of the King the youngest and dearest was to be sought out. They, however, resembled each other exactly, and were only to be distinguished by their having eaten different sweetmeats before they fell asleep: the eldest a bit of sugar; the second a little syrup; and the youngest a spoonful of honey. Then the Queen of the bees, which Simpleton had protected from the fire, came and tasted the lips of all three, and at last she remained sitting on the mouth which had eaten honey, and thus the King's son recognized the right princess. Then the enchantment was at an end; everything was released from sleep, and those who had been turned to stone received once more their natural forms. Simpleton married the youngest and sweetest princess. After her father's death he became King, and his two brothers received the two other sisters.

Amongst the three sleeping daughters of the King was the youngest
and dearest to be sought out

THE GOLDEN GOOSE

There was a man who had three sons, the youngest of whom was called the Simpleton, and was despised, laughed at, and neglected, on every occasion. It happened one day that the eldest son wished to go into the forest to cut wood, and before he went his mother gave him a delicious pancake and a flask of wine, that he might not suffer from hunger or thirst. When he came into the forest a little old gray man met him, who wished him good day, and said, "Give me a bit of cake out of your pocket, and let me have a drink of your wine; I am so hungry and thirsty."

But the prudent youth answered, "Give you my cake and my wine? I haven't got any; be off with you." And leaving the little man standing there, he went off.

Then he began to fell a tree, but he had not been at it long before he made a wrong stroke, and the hatchet hit him in the arm, so that he was obliged to go home and get it bound up. That was what came of the little gray man.

Afterwards the second son went into the wood, and the mother gave to him, as to the eldest, a pancake and a flask of wine. The little old gray man met him also, and begged for a little bit of cake and a drink of wine. But the second son spoke out plainly, saying, "What I give you I lose myself, so be off with you." And leaving the little man standing there, he went off.

The punishment followed. As he was chopping away at the tree, he hit himself in the leg so severely that he had to be carried home.

Then said the Simpleton, "Father, let me go for once into the forest to cut wood"; and the father answered, "Your brothers have hurt themselves by so doing; give it up, you understand nothing about it."

But the Simpleton went on begging so long, that the father said at last, "Well, be off with you; you will only learn by experience."

The mother gave him a cake (it was only made with water, and baked in the ashes), and with it a flask of sour beer. When he came into the forest the little old gray man met him, and greeted him, saying, "Give me a bit of your cake, and a drink from your flask; I am so hungry and thirsty."

And the Simpleton answered, "I have only a flour and water cake and sour beer; but if that is good enough for you, let us sit down together and

Yonder stands an old tree; cut it down, and at its roots you will find something.

eat." Then they sat down, and as the Simpleton took out his flour and water cake it became a rich pancake, and his sour beer became good wine.

Then they ate and drank, and afterwards the little man said, "As you have such a kind heart, and shared what you have so willingly, I will bestow good luck upon you. Yonder stands an old tree; cut it down, and at its roots you will find something," and thereupon the little man took his departure.

The Simpleton went there, and hewed away at the tree, and when it fell he saw, sitting among the roots, a goose with feathers of pure gold. He lifted it out and took it with him to an inn where he intended to stay the night.

The landlord had three daughters who, when they saw the goose, were curious to know what wonderful kind of bird it was, and ended by longing for one of its golden feathers. The eldest thought, "I will wait for a good opportunity, and then I will pull out one of its feathers for myself; and so, when the Simpleton was gone out, she seized the goose by its wing—but

there her finger and hand had to stay, held fast. Soon after came the second
sister with the same idea of plucking out one of the golden feathers for
herself; but scarcely had she touched her sister than she also was obliged to
stay, held fast. Lastly came the third with the same intentions; but the others
screamed out, "Stay away! for heaven's sake stay away!" But she did not see
why she should stay away, and thought, "If they do so, why should not I?"
and went towards them. But when she reached her sisters there she stopped,
hanging on with them. And so they had to stay, all night.

The next morning the Simpleton took the goose under his arm and went
away, unmindful of the three girls that hung on to it. The three had to run
after him, left and right, wherever his legs carried him. In the midst of the
fields they met the parson, who, when he saw the procession, said, "Shame
on you, girls, running after a young fellow through the fields like this," and
forthwith he seized hold of the youngest by the hand to drag her away, but
hardly had he touched her when he too was obliged to run after them himself.

Not long after the sexton came that way, and seeing the respected parson
following at the heels of the three girls, he called out, "Ho, your reverence,
whither away so quickly? You forget that we have another christening today";
and he seized hold of him by his gown; but no sooner had he touched him
than he was obliged to follow on too. As the five tramped on, one after
another, two peasants with their hoes came up from the fields, and the parson

And now there were seven following the Simpleton and the goose

cried out to them, and begged them to come and set him and the sexton free, but no sooner had they touched the sexton than they had to follow on too; and now there were seven following the Simpleton and the goose.

By and by they came to a town where a King reigned, who had an only daughter who was so serious that no one could make her laugh; therefore the King had given out that whoever should make her laugh should have her in marriage. The Simpleton, when he heard this, went with his goose and his hangers-on into the presence of the King's daughter, and as soon as she saw the seven people following always one after the other, she burst out laughing, and seemed as if she could never stop. And so the Simpleton earned a right to her as his bride; but the King did not like him for a son-in-law and made all kinds of objections, and said he must first bring a man who could drink up a whole cellar of wine.

The Simpleton thought that the little gray man would be able to help him, and went out into the forest, and there, on the very spot where he felled the tree, he saw a man sitting with a very sad countenance. The Simpleton asked him what was the matter, and he answered, "I have a great thirst, which I cannot quench: cold water does not agree with me; I have indeed drunk up a whole cask of wine, but what good is a drop like that?"

Then said the Simpleton, "I can help you; only come with me, and you shall have enough."

He took him straight to the King's cellar, and the man sat himself down before the big vats, and drank, and drank, and before a day was over he had drunk up the whole cellar-full.

As soon as she saw the seven people following always
one after the other, she burst out laughing

The Simpleton again asked for his bride, but the King was annoyed that a wretched fellow, called the Simpleton by everybody, should carry off his daughter, and so he made new conditions. He was to produce a man who could eat up a mountain of bread. The Simpleton did not hesitate long, but ran quickly off to the forest, and there in the same place sat a man who had fastened a strap round his body, making a very piteous face, and saying, "I have eaten a whole bakehouse full of rolls, but what is the use of that when one is so hungry as I am? My stomach feels quite empty, and I am obliged to strap myself together, that I may not die of hunger."

The Simpleton was quite glad of this, and said, "Get up quickly, and come along with me, and you shall have enough to eat."

He led him straight to the King's courtyard, where all the meal in the kingdom had been collected and baked into a mountain of bread. The man out of the forest settled himself down before it and hastened to eat, and in one day the whole mountain had disappeared.

Then the Simpleton asked for his bride the third time. The King, however, found one more excuse, and said he must have a ship that should be able to sail on land or on water. "So soon," said he, "as you come sailing along with it, you shall have my daughter for your wife."

The Simpleton went straight to the forest, and there sat the little old gray man with whom he had shared his cake, and he said, "I have eaten for you, and I have drunk for you, I will also give you the ship; and all because you were kind to me at the first."

The king knew he could no longer withhold his daughter

Then he gave him the ship that could sail on land and on water, and when the King saw it he knew that he could no longer withhold his daughter. The marriage took place immediately, and at the death of the King the Simpleton possessed the kingdom, and lived long and happily with his wife.

JORINDA AND JORINDEL

There was once an old castle in the middle of a deep wood, and in it an old woman who was a witch lived all by herself. In the daytime she changed into a cat or a screech-owl, but in the evening she took her proper shape again as a human being. She lured wild beasts and birds to her, and then she killed and boiled and roasted them.

If anyone came within one hundred steps of the castle he must needs stand still, and then he could not stir from the place until she bade him be free. But whenever a young maid came within this circle, the woman changed her into a bird, and shut her up in a wicker-work cage, and carried the cage into a room in the castle. She had about seven thousand cages of rare birds in the castle.

In the daytime she was changed into a cat

The owl flew into the thicket

Now there was once a maiden who was named Jorinda, who was fairer than all other girls. She and a handsome youth named Jorindel had promised to marry each other, and their greatest happiness was in being together. One day, in order that they might be able to talk together in quiet, they went for a walk in the forest.

"Take care," said Jorindel, " that you do not go too near the castle." It was at the end of a beautiful day; the sun shot its beams between the trunks of the trees, and the turtle-doves sang mournfully upon the young boughs of the birch-trees.

Jorinda wept now and then: she did not know why; the sun was low in the west, and a sadness came over her. Jorindel was sorrowful too; they were as sad as if they were about to die. Then they looked around them, and were quite at a loss, for they did not know by which way they should go home. The sun was still half above the mountain, but the other half was set.

Jorindel looked through the bushes, and saw they were close by the old castle. He was filled with deadly fear. Jorinda was singing—

> My little bird, with the necklace red,
> Sings sorrow, sorrow, sorrow,
> He sings that the dove must soon be dead,
> Sings sorrow, sor—Jug, jug, jug.

Jorindel looked for Jorinda. She was changed into a nightingale, and sang "jug, jug, jug." A screech-owl with glowing eyes flew three times round about her, and three times cried "to-whoo, to-whoo, to-whoo!"

Jorindel could not move: he stood there like a stone, and could neither weep nor speak, nor move hand or foot.

The sun had now set. The owl flew into the thicket, and at once there came out of it a crooked old woman, yellow and lean, with large red eyes and a hooked nose, the point of which reached to her chin. She muttered to herself, caught the nightingale, and took it away in her hand.

Jorindel could neither speak nor move from the spot; the nightingale was gone. At last the woman came back, and said in a hollow voice—

"Greet thee, Zachiel. If the moon shines on the cage, Zachiel, let him loose at once." Then Jorindel was freed. He fell on his knees before the woman and begged that she would give him back his Jorinda, but she said

At last the woman came back, and said in a hollow voice—"Greet thee, Zachiel."

that he should never have her again, and went away. He called, he wept, but all in vain.

"Ah, what is to become of me?"

Jorindel went away, and at last came to a strange village; there he kept sheep for a long time. He often walked round and round the castle, but not too near it. At last he dreamt one night that he found a blood-red flower, and in the middle of it was a beautiful large pearl; he dreamt again that he picked the flower and went with it to the castle, and that everything he touched with the flower was freed from enchantment; he also dreamt that by means of it he set his Jorinda free.

In the morning, when he awoke, he began to seek over hill and dale for the flower he had seen in his dream. Seven days he sought for it, and then, early in the morning, he found the blood-red flower. In the middle of it there was a large dewdrop, as big as the finest pearl.

Day and night he went on his way with this flower to the castle. When he was within a hundred steps of it he was not held fast, but walked on to the door. Jorindel was full of joy; he touched the door with the flowera and it sprang open. He walked in through the courtyard, and listened for the sound of the birds. At last he heard it. He went on, and found the room from whence it came, and there the witch was feeding the birds in the seven thousand cages.

When she saw Jorindel she was angry, very angry, and scolded, but she could not come within two steps of him. He did not take any notice of her, but went and looked at the cages with the birds; but there were many hundred nightingales; how was he to find his Jorinda again?

Just then he saw the old woman quietly take away a cage with a bird in it and go toward the door.

Swiftly he sprang toward her, and touched her and the cage with the flower. The woman could no longer bewitch any one; and Jorinda was standing there, clasping him round the neck, and she was as beautiful as ever!

SNOW WHITE AND THE SEVEN DWARFS

Once upon a time in the middle of winter, when the flakes of snow were falling like feathers from the sky, a queen sat at a window sewing, and the frame of the window was made of black ebony. And whilst she was sewing and looking out of the window at the snow, she pricked her finger with the needle, and three drops of blood fell upon the snow. And the red looked pretty upon the white snow, and she thought to herself, "Would that I had a child as white as snow, as red as blood, and as black as the wood of the window-frame."

Soon after that she had a little daughter, who was as white as snow, and as red as blood, and her hair was as black as ebony: and she was therefore called Little Snow White. And when the child was born, the Queen died.

After a year had passed the King took to himself another wife. She was a beautiful woman, but proud and haughty, and she could not bear that anyone else should surpass her in beauty. She had a wonderful looking-glass, and when she stood in front of it and looked at herself in it, and said—

> Looking-glass, looking-glass, on the wall,
> Who in this land is the fairest of all?

the looking-glass answered—

> Thou, O Queen, art the fairest of all!

Then she was satisfied, for she knew that the looking-glass spoke the truth.

But Snow White was growing up, and grew more and more beautiful; and when she was seven years old she was as beautiful as the day, and more beautiful than the Queen herself. And once when the Queen asked her looking-glass—

> Looking-glass, looking-glass, on the wall,
> Who in this land is the fairest of all?

it answered—

Thou art fairer than all who are here, Lady Queen.
But more beautiful still is Snow White, as I ween.

Then the Queen was shocked, and turned yellow and green with envy.
From that hour, whenever she looked at Snow White, her heart heaved in
her breast, she hated the girl so much.

And envy and pride grew higher and higher in her heart like a weed,
so that she had no peace day or night. She called a huntsman, and said, "
Take the child away into the forest; I will no longer have her in my sight.
Kill her, and bring me back her heart as a token."

The huntsman obeyed, and took her away; but when he had drawn his
knife, and was about to pierce Snow White's innocent heart, she began to
weep, and said, "Ah, dear hunts-
man, leave me my life! I will run
away into the wild forest, and
never come home again."

And as she was so beautiful
the huntsman had pity on her and
told her to run away. "The wild
beasts will soon have devoured
you," thought he, and yet it seemed
as if a stone had been rolled from
his heart since it was no longer
needful for him to kill her. And
as a young boar just then came
running by he stabbed it, and cut
out its heart and took it to the
Queen as proof that the child was
dead. The cook had to salt this,
and the wicked Queen ate it, and
thought she had eaten the heart
of Snow White.

But now the poor child was
all alone in the great forest, and
so terrified that she looked at
every leaf of every tree, and did

*"Looking-glass, looking-glass, on the wall, who
in this land is the fairest of all?"*

not know what to do. Then she began to run, and ran over sharp stones and through thorns, and the wild beasts ran past her, but did her no harm. She ran as long as her feet would go until it was almost evening; then she saw a little cottage and went into it to rest herself. Everything in the cottage was small, but neater and cleaner than can be told. There was a table on which was a white cover, and seven little plates, and on each plate a little spoon; moreover, there were seven little knives and forks, and seven little mugs. Against the wall stood seven little beds side by side, and covered with snow white counterpanes.

Little Snow White was so hungry and thirsty that she ate some vegetables and bread from each plate and drank a drop of wine out of each mug, for she did not wish to take all from one only. Then, as she was so tired, she laid herself down on one of the little beds, but none of them suited her; one was too long, another too short, but at last she found that the seventh one was right, and so she remained in it, said a prayer and went to sleep.

When it was quite dark the owners of the cottage came back; they were seven dwarfs who dug and delved in the mountains for ore. They lit their seven candles, and as it was now light within the cottage they saw that someone had been there, for everything was not in the same order in which they had left it.

The first said, "Who has been sitting on my chair?"

The second, "Who has been eating off my plate?"

The third, "Who has been taking some of my bread?"

The fourth, "Who has been eating my vegetables?"

The fifth, "Who has been using my fork?"

The sixth, "Who has been cutting with my knife?"

The seventh, "Who has been drinking out of my mug?"

Then the first looked round and saw that there was a little hole on his bed, and he said, "Who has been getting into my bed?" The others came up and each called out, "Somebody has been lying in my bed too." But the seventh when he looked at his bed saw little Snow White, who was lying asleep therein. And he called the others, who came running up, and they cried out with astonishment, and brought their seven little candles and let the light fall on little Snow White.

"Oh, heavens! oh, heavens!" cried they, "what a lovely child!" and they were so glad that they did not wake her up, but let her sleep on in the bed. And the seventh dwarf slept with his companions, one hour with each, and so got through the night.

When it was quite dark the owners of the cottage came back

When it was morning little Snow White awoke, and was frightened when she saw the seven dwarfs. But they were friendly and asked her what her name was. "My name is Snow White," she answered. "How have you come to our house?" said the dwarfs. Then she told them that her stepmother had wished to have her killed, but that the huntsman had spared her life, and that she had run for the whole day, until at last she had found their dwelling.

The dwarfs said, "If you will take care of our house, cook, make the beds, wash, sew, and knit, and if you will keep everything neat and clean, you can stay with us and you shall want for nothing."

"Yes," said Snow White, "with all my heart," and she stayed with them. She kept the house in order for them; in the mornings they went to the mountains and looked for copper and gold, in the evenings they came back, and then their supper had to be ready. The girl was alone the whole day, so the good dwarfs warned her and said, "Beware of your stepmother, she will soon know that you are here; be sure to let no one come in."

But the Queen, believing that she had eaten Snow White's heart, could not but think that she was again the first and most beautiful of all; and she went to her looking-glass and said—

> Looking-glass, looking-glass, on the wall,
> Who in this land is the fairest of all?

and the glass answered —

> Oh, Queen, thou art fairest of all I see,
> But over the hills, where the seven dwarfs dwell,
> Snow White is still alive and well,
> And none is so fair as she.

Then she was astounded, for she knew that the looking-glass never spoke falsely, and she knew that the huntsman had betrayed her, and that little Snow White was still alive.

And so she thought and thought again how she might kill her, for so long as she was not the fairest in the whole land, envy let her have no rest. And when she had at last thought of something to do, she painted her face, and dressed herself like an old peddler-woman, and no one could have known her. In this disguise she went over the seven mountains to the seven dwarfs, and knocked at the door and cried, "Pretty things to sell, very cheap, very cheap."

Little Snow White looked out of the window and called out, "Good-day my good woman, what have you to sell?"

"Good things, pretty things," she answered; "stay-laces of all colors," and she pulled out one which was woven of bright-colored silk.

"I may let the worthy old woman in," thought Snow White, and she unbolted the door and bought the pretty laces.

"Child," said the old woman, "what a fright you look; come, I will lace you properly for once."

Snow White had no suspicion, but stood before her, and let herself be laced with the new laces. But the old woman laced so quickly and so tightly that Snow White lost her breath and fell down as if dead.

"Now I am the most beautiful," said the Queen to herself, and ran away.

Not long afterwards, in the evening, the seven dwarfs came home, but how shocked they were when they saw their dear little Snow White lying on the ground, and that she neither stirred nor moved, and seemed to be dead. They lifted her up, and, as they saw that she was laced too tightly, they cut the laces; then she began to breathe a little, and after a while came to life again. When the dwarfs heard what had happened they said, "The old peddler-woman was no one else than the wicked Queen; take care and let no one come in when we are not with you."

But the wicked woman when she had reached home went in front of the glass and asked—

> Looking-glass, looking-glass, on the wall,
> Who in this land is the fairest of all?

and it answered as before—

> Oh, Queen, thou art fairest of all I see,
> But over the hills, where the seven dwarfs dwell,
> Snow White is still alive and well,
> And none is so fair as she.

When she heard that, all her blood rushed to her heart with fear, for she saw plainly that little Snow White was again alive. "But now," she said, "I will think of something that shall put an end to you," and by the help of witchcraft, which she understood, she made a poisonous comb.

Then she disguised herself and took the shape of another old woman. So she went over the seven mountains to the seven dwarfs, knocked at the door, and cried, "Good things to sell, cheap, cheap!"

Little Snow White looked out and said, "Go away; I cannot let any one come in."

"I suppose you can look," said the old woman, and pulled the poisonous comb out and held it up. It pleased the girl so well that she let herself be beguiled, and opened the door.

When they had made a bargain the old woman said, "Now I will comb you properly for once." Poor little Snow White had no suspicion, and let the old woman do as she pleased, but hardly had she put the comb in her hair than the poison in it took effect, and the girl fell down senseless. "You paragon of beauty," said the wicked woman, "you are done for now," and she went away.

But fortunately it was almost evening, when the seven dwarfs came home. When they saw Snow White lying as if dead upon the ground they at once suspected the stepmother, and they looked and found the poisoned comb. Scarcely had they taken it out when Snow White came to herself, and told them what had happened. Then they warned her once more to be upon her guard and to open the door to no one.

The Queen, at home, went in front of the glass and said—

> Looking-glass, looking-glass, on the wall,
> Who in this land is the fairest of all?

then it answered as before—

> Oh, Queen, thou art fairest of all I see,
> But over the hills, where the seven dwarfs dwell,
> Snow White is still alive and well,
> And none is so fair as she.

When she heard the glass speak thus she trembled and shook with rage. "Snow White shall die," she cried, "even if it costs me my life!"

Thereupon she went into a quite secret, lonely room, where no one ever came, and there she made a very poisonous apple. Outside it looked pretty, white with a red cheek, so that everyone who saw it longed for it; but whoever ate a piece of it must surely die. When the apple was ready she painted her face, and dressed herself up as a country-woman, and so she went over the seven mountains to the seven dwarfs. She knocked at the door.

Snow White put her head out of the window and said, "I cannot let any one in; the seven dwarfs have forbidden me."

"It is all the same to me," answered the woman, "I shall soon get rid of my apples. There, I will give you one."

"No," said Snow White, "I dare not take anything."

"Are you afraid of poison?" said the old woman. "Look, I will cut the apple in two pieces; you eat the red cheek, and I will eat the white." The apple was so cunningly made that only the red cheek was poisoned. Snow White longed for the fine apple, and when she saw that the woman ate part of it she could resist no longer, and stretched out her hand and took the poisonous half. But hardly had she a bit of it in her mouth than she fell down dead. Then the Queen looked at her with a dreadful look, and laughed aloud and said, "White as snow, red as blood, black as ebony-wood! This time the dwarfs cannot wake you up again."

And when she asked of the looking-glass at home—

Looking-glass, looking-glass, on the wall,
Who in this land is the fairest of all?

it answered at last—

Oh, Queen, in this land thou art fairest of all.

Then her envious heart had rest, so far as an envious heart can have rest.

The dwarfs, when they came home in the evening, found Snow White lying upon the ground; she breathed no longer and was dead. They lifted her up, looked to see whether they could find anything poisonous, unlaced her, combed her hair, washed her with water and wine, but it was all of no use; the poor child was dead, and remained dead. They laid her upon a bier, and all seven of them sat round it and wept for her, and wept three days long.

Then they were going to bury her, but she still looked as if she were living, and still had her pretty red cheeks. They said, "We could not bury her in the dark ground," and they had a transparent coffin of glass made, so that she could be seen from all sides, and they laid her in it, and wrote her name upon it in golden letters, and that she was a king's daughter. Then they put the coffin out upon the mountain, and one of them always stayed by it and watched it. And birds came too, and wept for Snow White; first an owl, then a raven, and last a dove.

And now Snow White lay a long, long time in the coffin, and she did not change, but looked as if she were asleep; for she was as white as snow, as red as blood, and her hair was as black as ebony.

It happened, however, that a king's son came into the forest, and went to the dwarf's house to spend the night. He saw the coffin on the mountain, and the beautiful Snow White within it, and read what was written upon it

The dwarfs, when they came home in the evening, found Snow White lying upon the ground

in golden letters. Then he said to the dwarfs, "Let me have the coffin, I will give you whatever you want for it."

But the dwarfs answered, "We will not part with it for all the gold in the world."

Then he said, "Let me have it as a gift, for I cannot live without seeing Snow White. I will honor and prize her as my dearest possession." As he spoke in this way the good dwarfs took pity upon him, and gave him the coffin.

And now the King's son had it carried away by his servants on their shoulders. And it happened that they stumbled over a tree-stump, and with the shock the poisonous piece of apple which Snow White had bitten off came out of her throat. And before long she opened her eyes, lifted up the lid of the coffin, sat up, and was once more alive.

"Oh, heavens, where am I?" she cried.

The King's son, full of joy, said, "You are with me," and told her what had happened, and said, "I love you more than everything in the world; come with me to my father's palace, you shall be my wife."

And Snow White was willing, and went with him, and their wedding was held with great show and splendor. But Snow White's wicked stepmother was also bidden to the feast. When she had arrayed herself in beautiful clothes she went before the looking-glass, and said—

> Looking-glass, looking-glass, on the wall,
> Who in this land is the fairest of all?

the glass answered—

> Oh, Queen, of all here the fairest art thou,
> But the young Queen is fairer by far as I trow.

Then the wicked woman uttered a curse, and was so wretched, so utterly wretched, that she knew not what to do. At first she would not go to the wedding at all, but she had no peace, and must go to see the young Queen. And when she went in she knew Snow White; and she stood still with rage and fear, and could not stir. But iron slippers had already been put upon the fire, and they were brought in with tongs, and set before her. Then she was forced to put on the red-hot shoes, and dance until she dropped down dead.

THE SHOES THAT WERE DANCED TO PIECES

There was once upon a time a King who had twelve daughters, each one more beautiful than the other. They all slept together in one chamber, in which their beds stood side by side, and every night when they were in them the King locked the door and bolted it. In the morning, when he unlocked the door, he saw that their shoes were worn out with dancing, and no one could find out how that had come to pass. Then the King caused it to be proclaimed that whosoever could discover where they danced at night should choose one of them for his wife and be King after his death; but that whosoever came forward and had not discovered it within three days and nights, should have forfeited his life.

It was not long before a King's son presented himself, and offered to undertake the enterprise. He was well received, and in the evening was led into a room adjoining the princesses' sleeping-chamber. His bed was placed there, and he was to observe where they went and danced, and in order that they might do nothing secretly or go away to some other place, the door of their room was left open.

But the eyelids of the prince grew heavy as lead, and he fell asleep, and when he awoke in the morning, all twelve had been to the dance, for their shoes were standing there with holes in the soles. On the second and third nights it fell out just the same, and then his head was struck off without mercy. Many others came after this and undertook the enterprise, but all forfeited their lives.

Now it came to pass that a poor soldier, who had a wound, and could serve no longer, found himself on the road to the town where the King lived. There he met an old woman, who asked him where he was going.

"I hardly know myself," answered he, and added in jest, "I had half a mind to discover where the princesses danced their shoes into holes, and thus become King."

"That is not so difficult," said the old woman. "You must not drink the wine which will be brought to you at night, and must pretend to be sound asleep."

With that she gave him a little cloak, and said, "If you put on that, you will be invisible, and then you can steal after the twelve." When the soldier had received this good advice, he went into the thing in earnest, took heart, went to the King, and announced himself as a suitor. He was as well received as the others, and royal garments were put upon him. He was conducted that evening at bedtime into the antechamber, and as he was about to go to bed, the eldest came and brought him a cup of wine, but he had tied a sponge under his chin, and let the wine run down into it, without drinking a drop. Then he lay down and when he had lain a while, he began to snore, as if in the deepest sleep.

The twelve princesses heard that, and laughed, and the eldest said, "He, too, might as well have saved his life." With that they got up, opened wardrobes, presses, cupboards, and brought out pretty dresses; dressed themselves before the mirrors, sprang about, and rejoiced at the prospect of the dance.

Only the youngest said, "I know not how it is; you are very happy, but I feel very strange; some misfortune is certainly about to befall us."

"Thou art a goose, who art always frightened," said the eldest. "Hast thou forgotten how many Kings' sons have already come here in vain? I had hardly any need to give the soldier a sleeping-draught, in any case the clown would not have awakened."

When they were all ready they looked carefully at the soldier, but he had closed his eyes and did not move or stir, so they felt themselves quite secure. The eldest then went to her bed and tapped it; it immediately sank into the earth, and one after the other they descended through the opening, the eldest going first.

The soldier, who had watched everything, tarried no longer, put on his little cloak, and went down last with the youngest. Half-way down the steps, he just trod a little on her dress; she was terrified at that, and cried out, "What is that? Who is pulling my dress?"

"Don't be so silly!" said the eldest, "you have caught it on a nail."

Then they went all the way down, and when they were at the bottom, they were standing in a wonderfully pretty avenue of trees, all the leaves of which were of silver, and shone and glistened. The soldier thought, "I must carry a token away with me," and broke off a twig from one of them, on which the tree cracked with a loud report.

The youngest cried out again. "Something is wrong, did you hear the crack?"

But the eldest said, "It is a gun fired for joy, because we have got rid of our prince so quickly."

After that they came into an avenue where all the leaves were of gold, and lastly into a third where they were of bright diamonds; he broke off a twig from each, which made such a crack each time that the youngest started back in terror, but the eldest still maintained that they were salutes. They went on and came to a great lake whereon stood twelve little boats, and in every boat sat a handsome prince, all of whom were waiting for the twelve, and each took one of them with him, but the soldier seated himself by the youngest.

Then her prince said, "I can't tell why the boat is so much heavier today; I shall have to row with all my strength, if I am to get it across."

"What should cause that," said the youngest, "but the warm weather? I feel very warm too."

On the opposite side of the lake stood a splendid, brightly-lit castle, from whence resounded the joyous music of trumpets and kettle-drums. They rowed over there, entered, and each prince danced with the girl he loved, but the soldier danced with them unseen, and when one of them had a cup of wine in her hand he drank it up, so that the cup was empty when she carried it to her mouth; the youngest was alarmed at this, but the eldest always made her be silent.

They danced there till three o'clock in the morning when all the shoes were danced into holes, and they were forced to leave off; the princes rowed them back again over the lake, and this time the soldier seated himself by the eldest. On the shore they took leave of their princes, and promised to return the following night.

When they reached the stairs the soldier ran on in front and lay down in his bed, and when the twelve had come up slowly and wearily, he was already

On the opposite side of the lake stood a splendid, brightly-lit castle

snoring so loudly that they could all hear him, and they said, "So far as he is concerned, we are safe." They took off their beautiful dresses, laid them away, put the worn-out shoes under the bed, and lay down. Next morning the soldier was resolved not to speak, but to watch the wonderful goings on, and again went with them.

Then everything was done just as it had been done the first time, and each time they danced until their shoes were worn to pieces. But the third time he took a cup away with him as a token. When the hour had arrived for him to give his answer, he took the three twigs and the cup, and went to the King, but the twelve stood behind the door, and listened for what he was going to say. When the King put the question, "Where have my twelve daughters danced their shoes to pieces in the night?" he answered, "In an underground castle with twelve princes," and related how it had come to pass, and brought out the tokens.

The King then summoned his daughters, and asked them if the soldier had told the truth. When they saw that they were betrayed, and that falsehood would be of no avail, they were obliged to confess all. Thereupon the King asked which of them he would have to wife? He answered, "I am no longer young, so give me the eldest." Then the wedding was celebrated on the self-same day, and the kingdom was promised him after the King's death. But the princes were bewitched for as many days as they had danced nights with the twelve.

THE OLD MAN AND HIS GRANDSON

There was once a very old man, whose eyes had become dim, his ears dull of hearing, his knees trembled, and when he sat at table he could hardly hold the spoon, and spilt the broth upon the table-cloth or let it run out of his mouth. His son and his son's wife were disgusted at this, so the old grandfather was made to sit in the corner behind the stove, and they gave him his food in an earthenware bowl, and not even enough of it. And he used to look towards the table with his eyes full of tears.

*The old grandfather was made to sit in the corner behind the stove,
and they gave him his food in an earthenware bowl*

Once, too, his trembling hands could not hold the bowl, and it fell to the ground and broke. The young wife scolded him, but he said nothing and only sighed. Then they bought him a wooden bowl for a few half-pence, out of which he had to eat.

They were once sitting thus when the little grandson of four years old began to gather together some bits of wood upon the ground. "What are you doing there?" asked the father. "I am making a little trough," answered the child, "for father and mother to eat out of when I am big."

The man and his wife looked at each other for a while, and presently began to cry. Then they took the old grandfather to the table, and henceforth always let him eat with them, and likewise said nothing if he did spill a little of anything.

THE VALIANT LITTLE TAILOR

One summer's morning a little tailor was sitting at his table by the window. He was in good spirits, and sewed with all his might. Then came a peasant woman down the street crying, "Good jams, cheap! Good jams, cheap!"

This rang pleasantly in the tailor's ears; he stretched his delicate head out of the window, and called, "Come up here, dear woman; here you will get rid of your goods."

The woman came up the three steps to the tailor with her heavy basket, and he made her unpack the whole of the pots for him. He inspected all of them, lifted them up, put his nose to them, and at length said, "The jam seems to me to be good, so weigh me out four ounces, dear woman, and if it is a quarter of a pound that is of no consequence."

The woman who had hoped to find a good sale, gave him what he desired, but went away quite angry and grumbling.

"Now, God bless the jam to my use," cried the little tailor, "and give me health and strength"; so he brought the bread out of the cupboard, cut himself a piece right across the loaf and spread the jam over it. "This won't taste bitter," said he, "but I will just finish the jacket before I take a bite." He laid the bread near him, sewed on, and in his joy, made bigger and bigger stitches. In the meantime the smell of the sweet jam ascended so to the wall, where the flies were sitting in great numbers, that they were attracted and descended on it in hosts.

"Hola! who invited you?" said the little tailor, and drove the unbidden guests away. The flies, however, who understood no German, would not be turned away, but came back again in ever-increasing companies. The little tailor at last lost all patience, and got a bit of cloth from the hole under his work-table, and saying, "Wait, and I will give it to you," struck it mercilessly on them. When he drew it away and counted, there lay before him no fewer than seven, dead and with legs stretched out. "Art thou a fellow of that sort?" said he, and could not help admiring his own bravery. "The whole town shall know of this!"

And the little tailor hastened to cut himself a girdle, stitched it, and embroidered on it in large letters, "Seven at one stroke!" "What, the town!" he continued, "The whole world shall hear of it!" and his heart wagged with joy like a lamb's tail.

The tailor put on the girdle, and resolved to go forth into the world, because he thought his workshop was too small for his

"Wait and I will give it to you."

valor. Before he went away, he sought about in the house to see if there was anything which he could take with him; however, he found nothing but an old cheese, and that he put in his pocket. In front of the door he observed a bird which had caught itself in the thicket. It had to go into his pocket with the cheese. Now he took to the road boldly, and as he was light and nimble, he felt no fatigue.

The road led him up a mountain, and when he had reached the highest point of it, there sat a powerful giant looking about him quite comfortably. The little tailor went bravely up, spoke to him, and said, "Good day, comrade, so thou art sitting there overlooking the wide-spread world! I am just on my way thither, and want to try my luck. Hast thou any inclination to go with me?"

The giant looked contemptuously at the tailor, and said, "Thou ragamuffin! Thou miserable creature!"

"Oh, indeed?" answered the little tailor, and unbuttoned his coat, and showed the giant the girdle, "There mayst thou read what kind of a man I am!"

The giant read, "Seven at one stroke," and thought that they had been men whom the tailor had killed, and began to feel a little respect for the tiny fellow. Nevertheless, he wished to try him first, and took a stone in his hand and squeezed it together so that water dropped out of it. "Do that likewise," said the giant, "if thou hast strength?"

"Is that all?" said the tailor, "that is child's play with us!" and put his hand into his pocket, brought out the soft cheese, and pressed it until the liquid ran out of it. "Faith," said he, "that was a little better, wasn't it?"

The giant did not know what to say, and could not believe it of the little man. Then the giant picked up a stone and threw it so high that the eye could scarcely follow it. "Now, little mite of a man, do that likewise."

"Well thrown," said the tailor, "but after all the stone came down to earth again; I will throw you one which shall never come back at all." And he put his hand into his pocket, took out the bird, and threw it into the air. The bird, delighted with its liberty, rose, flew away and did not come back. "How does that shot please you, comrade?" asked the tailor.

"Thou canst certainly throw," said the giant, "but now we will see if thou art able to carry anything properly."

He took the little tailor to a mighty oak tree which lay there felled on the ground, and said, "If thou art strong enough, help me to carry the tree out of the forest."

*. . . and put his hand into his pocket, brought out the soft cheese,
and pressed it until the liquid ran out of it*

"Readily," answered the little man; "take thou the trunk on thy shoulders, and I will raise up the branches and twigs; after all, they are the heaviest." The giant took the trunk on his shoulder, but the tailor seated himself on a branch, and the giant who could not look round, had to carry away the whole tree, and the little tailor into the bargain: he behind, was quite merry and happy, and whistled the song, *"Three tailors rode forth from the gate,"* as if carrying the tree were child's play. The giant, after he had dragged the heavy burden part of the way, could go no further, and cried, "Hark you, I shall have to let the tree fall!"

The tailor sprang nimbly down, seized the tree with both arms as if he had been carrying it, and said to the giant, "Thou art such a great fellow, and yet canst not even carry the tree!"

They went on together, and as they passed a cherry-tree, the giant laid hold of the top of the tree where the ripest fruit was hanging, bent it down, gave it into the tailor's hand, and bade him eat. But the little tailor was much too weak to hold the tree, and when the giant let it go, it sprang back again, and the tailor was hurried into the air with it. When he had fallen down again without injury, the giant said, "What is this? Hast thou not strength enough to hold the weak twig?"

"There is no lack of strength," answered the little tailor. "Dost thou think that could be anything to a man who has struck down seven at one blow? I leapt over the tree because the huntsmen are shooting down there in the thicket. Jump as I did, if thou canst do it."

The giant made the attempt, but could not get over the tree, and remained hanging in the branches, so that in this also the tailor kept the upper hand.

The giant said, "If thou art such a valiant fellow, come with me into our cavern and spend the night with us." The little tailor was willing, and followed him. When they went into the cave, other giants were sitting there by the fire, and each of them had a roasted sheep in his hand and was eating it. The little tailor looked round and thought, "It is much more spacious here than in my workshop."

The giant showed him a bed, and said he was to lie down in it and sleep. The bed, however, was too big for the little tailor; he did not lie down in it, but crept into a corner. When it was midnight, and the giant thought that the little tailor was lying in a sound sleep, he got up, took a great iron bar,

cut through the bed with one blow, and thought he had given the grass-
hopper his finishing stroke. With the earliest dawn the giants went into the
forest, and had quite forgotten the little tailor, when all at once he walked up
to them quite merrily and boldly. The giants were terrified, they were afraid
that he would strike them all dead, and ran away in a great hurry.

The little tailor went onwards, always following his own pointed nose.
After he had walked for a long time, he came to the courtyard of a royal
palace, and as he felt weary, he lay down on the grass and fell asleep. Whilst
he lay there, the people came and inspected him on all sides, and read on his
girdle, "Seven at one stroke."

"Ah," said they, "What does the great warrior here in the midst of peace?
He must be a mighty lord."

They went and announced him to the King, and gave it as their opinion
that if war should break out, this would be a weighty and useful man who
ought on no account to be allowed to depart. The counsel pleased the King,
and he sent one of his courtiers to the little tailor to offer him military service
when he awoke. The ambassador remained standing by the sleeper, waited
until he stretched his limbs and opened his eyes, and then conveyed to him
this proposal. "For this very reason have I come here," the tailor replied, "I am
ready to enter the King's service."

He was therefore honorably received and a special dwelling was assigned
him.

The soldiers, however, were set against the little tailor, and wished him
a thousand miles away. "What is to be the end of this?" they said amongst
themselves. "If we quarrel with him, and he strikes about him, seven of us
will fall at every blow; not one of us can stand against him."

They came therefore to a decision, betook themselves in a body to the
King, and begged for their dismissal. "We are not prepared," said they, "to stay
with a man who kills seven at one stroke."

The King was sorry that for the sake of one he should lose all his
faithful servants, wished that he had never set eyes on the tailor, and would
willingly have been rid of him again. But he did not venture to give him his
dismissal, for he dreaded lest he should strike him and all his people dead,
and place himself on the royal throne. He thought about it for a long time,
and at last found good counsel. He sent to the little tailor and caused him
to be informed that as he was such a great warrior, he had one request to

make to him. In a forest of his country lived two giants who caused great mischief with their robbing, murdering, ravaging, and burning, and no one could approach them without putting himself in danger of death. If the tailor conquered and killed these two giants, he would give him his only daughter to wife, and half of his kingdom as a dowry; likewise one hundred horsemen should go with him to assist him.

"That would indeed be a fine thing for a man like me!" thought the little tailor. "One is not offered a beautiful princess and half a kingdom every day of one's life!"

"Oh, yes," he replied, "I will soon subdue the giants, and do not require the help of the hundred horsemen to do it; he who can hit seven with one blow has no need to be afraid of two."

The little tailor went forth, and the hundred horsemen followed him. When he came to the outskirts of the forest, he said to his followers, "Just stay waiting here, I alone will soon finish off the giants."

Then he bounded into the forest and looked about right and left. After a while he perceived both giants. They lay sleeping under a tree, and snored so that the branches waved up and down. The little tailor, not idle, gathered two pocketsful of stones, and with these climbed up the tree. When he was halfway up, he slipped down by a branch, until he sat just above the sleepers, and then let one stone after another fall on the breast of one of the giants. For a long time the giant felt nothing, but at last he awoke, pushed his comrade, and said, "Why art thou knocking me?"

"Thou must be dreaming," said the other, "I am not knocking thee." They laid themselves down to sleep again, and then the tailor threw a stone down on the second.

"What is the meaning of this?" cried the other. "Why art thou pelting me?"

"I am not pelting thee," answered the first, growling.

They disputed about it for a time, but as they were weary they let the matter rest, and their eyes closed once more. The little tailor began his game again, picked out the biggest stone, and threw it with all his might on the breast of the first giant.

"That is too bad!" cried he, and sprang up like a madman, and pushed his companion against the tree until it shook. The other paid him back in the same coin, and they got into such a rage that they tore up trees and belabored

They got into such a rage that they tore up trees

each other so long, that at last they both fell down dead on the ground at the same time. Then the little tailor leaped down.

"It is a lucky thing," said he, "that they did not tear up the tree on which I was sitting, or I should have had to spring on to another like a squirrel; but we tailors are nimble."

He drew out his sword and gave each of them a couple of thrusts in the breast, and then went out to the horsemen and said, "The work is done; I have given both of them their finishing stroke, but it was hard work! They tore up trees in their sore need, and defended themselves with them, but all that is to no purpose when a man like myself comes, who can kill seven at one blow."

"But are you not wounded?" asked the horsemen. "You need not concern yourself about that," answered the tailor, "They have not bent one hair of mine."

The horsemen would not believe him, and rode into the forest; there they found the giants swimming in their blood, and all round about lay the torn-up trees.

The little tailor demanded of the King the promised reward. The King, however, repented of his promise, and again bethought himself how he could get rid of the hero. "Before thou receivest my daughter, and the half of my kingdom," said he to him, "thou must perform one more heroic deed. In the forest roams a unicorn which does great harm, and thou must catch it first."

"I fear one unicorn still less than two giants. Seven at one blow, is my kind of affair."

He took a rope and an ax with him, went forth into the forest, and again bade those who were sent with him to wait outside. He had not to seek long. The unicorn soon came towards him, and rushed directly on the tailor, as if it would spit him on his horn without more ceremony.

"Softly, softly; it can't be done as quickly as that," said he, and stood still and waited until the animal was quite close, and then sprang nimbly behind the tree. The unicorn ran against the tree with all its strength, and struck its horn so fast in the trunk that it had not strength enough to draw it out again, and thus it was caught.

"Now, I have got the bird," said the tailor, and came out from behind the tree and put the rope round its neck, and then with his ax he hewed the horn out of the tree, and when all was ready he led the beast away and took it to the King.

The King still would not give him the promised reward, and made a third demand. Before the wedding the tailor was to catch him a wild boar that made great havoc in the forest, and the huntsmen should give him their help.

"Willingly," said the tailor, "that is child's play!"

He did not take the huntsmen with him into the forest, and they were well pleased that he did not, for the wild boar had several times received them in such a manner that they had no inclination to lie in wait for him. When the boar perceived the tailor, it ran on him with foaming mouth and whetted tusks, and was about to throw him to the ground, but the active hero sprang into a chapel which was near, and up to the window at once, and in one bound out again. The boar ran in after him, but the tailor ran round outside and shut the door behind it, and then the raging beast, which was much too heavy and awkward to leap out of the window, was caught. The little tailor called the huntsmen thither that they might see the prisoner with their own eyes. The hero, however went to the King, who was now, whether he liked it or not, obliged to keep his promise, and gave him his daughter and the half of his kingdom. Had he known that it was no warlike hero, but a little tailor who was standing before him, it would have gone to his heart still more than it did. The wedding was held with great magnificence and small joy, and out of a tailor a king was made.

After some time the young Queen heard her husband say in his dreams at night, "Boy, make me the doublet, and patch the pantaloons, or else I will rap the yard-measure over thine ears."

Then she discovered in what state of life the young lord had been born, and next morning complained of her wrongs to her father, and begged him to help her to get rid of her husband, who was nothing else but a tailor. The King comforted her and said, "Leave thy bedroom door open this night, and my servants shall stand outside, and when he has fallen asleep shall go in, bind him, and take him on board a ship which shall carry him into the wide world."

The woman was satisfied with this; but the King's armor-bearer, who had heard all, was friendly with the young lord, and informed him of the whole plot.

"I'll put a screw into that business," said the little tailor.

At night he went to bed with his wife at the usual time, and when she thought that he had fallen asleep, she got up, opened the door, and then lay down again. The little tailor, who was only pretending to be asleep, began to cry out in a clear voice, "Boy, make me the doublet and patch me the pantaloons, or I will rap the yard-measure over thine ears. I smote seven at one blow. I killed two giants, I brought away one unicorn and caught a wild boar, and am I to fear those who are standing outside the room."

When these men heard the tailor speaking thus, they were overcome by a great dread, and ran as if the wild huntsman were behind them, and none of them would venture anything further against him.

So the little tailor was a king and remained one, to the end of his life.

❧

THE THREE LANGUAGES

There once lived in Switzerland an aged count whose only son was stupid and could learn nothing. Then said the father, "Hark thee, my son, I can get nothing into thy head, let me try as I will. Thou must go from hence. I will give thee into the care of a celebrated master, who shall see what he can do with thee."

The youth was sent into a strange town, and remained a whole year with the master. At the end of this time, he came home again, and his father asked, "Now, my son, what hast thou learned?"

"Father, I have learned what the dogs say when they bark."

"Lord have mercy on us!" cried the father; "is that all thou hast learned? I will send thee into another town, to another master."

The youth was taken thither, and stayed a year with this master likewise. When he came back the father again asked, "My son, what hast thou learned?"

He answered, "Father, I have learnt what the birds say."

Then the father fell into a rage and said, "Oh, thou lost man, thou hast spent precious time and learned nothing; art thou not ashamed to appear before mine eyes? I will send thee to a third master, but if thou learn nothing this time, also, I will no longer be thy father."

The youth remained a whole year with the third master also, and when he came home again, and his father inquired, "My son, what hast thou learned?"

He answered, "Dear father, I have this year learned what the frogs croak."

Then the father fell into the most furious anger, sprang up, called his people thither, and said, "This man is no longer my son, I drive him forth, and command you to take him out into the forest, and kill him."

They took him forth, but when they should have killed him, they could not do it for pity, and let him go. And they cut the eyes and the tongue out of a deer that they might carry them to the old man as tokens.

The youth wandered on, and after some time came to a fortress where he begged for a night's lodging. "Yes," said the lord of the castle, "if thou wilt pass the night down there in the old tower, go thither. But I warn thee, it is at the peril of thy life, for it is full of wild dogs, which bark and howl without stopping, and at certain hours a man has to be given to them, whom they at once devour."

The whole district was in sorrow and dismay because of them, and yet no one could do anything to stop this. The youth, however, was without fear, and said, "Just let me go down to the barking dogs, and give me something that I can throw to them. They will do nothing to harm me."

As he himself would have it so, they gave him some food for the wild animals, and led him down to the tower. When he went inside, the dogs did not bark at him, but wagged their tails quite amicably around him, ate what he set before them, and did not hurt one hair of his head. Next morning, to the astonishment of everyone, he came out again safe and unharmed, and said to the lord of the castle, "The dogs have revealed to me, in their own language, why they dwell there, and bring evil on the land. They are bewitched, and are obliged to watch over a great treasure which is below in the tower, and they can have no rest until it is taken away. I have likewise learnt, from their discourse, how that is to be done."

Then all who heard this rejoiced, and the lord of the castle said he would adopt him as a son if he accomplished it successfully. He went down again, and as he knew what he had to do, he did it thoroughly, and brought a chest full of gold out with him. The howling of the wild dogs was henceforth heard no more; they had disappeared, and the country was freed from the trouble.

After some time he took it into his head that he would travel to Rome. On the way he passed by a marsh, in which a number of frogs were sitting croaking. He listened to them, and when he became aware of what they were saying, he grew very thoughtful and sad. At last he arrived in Rome, where the Pope had just died, and there was great difficulty as to whom they should appoint as his successor. They at length agreed that the person should be chosen as pope who should be distinguished by some divine and miraculous token.

On the way he passed by a marsh, in which a number of frogs were sitting croaking

And just as that was decided on, the young count entered into the church, and suddenly two snow white doves flew on his shoulders and remained sitting there. The ecclesiastics recognized therein the token from above, and asked him on the spot if he would be pope. He was undecided, and knew not if he were worthy of this, but the doves counseled him to do it, and at length he said yes. Then was he anointed and consecrated, and thus was fulfilled what he had heard from the frogs on his way, which had so affected him, that he was to be his Holiness the Pope. Then he had to sing a mass, and did not know one word of it, but the two doves sat continually on his shoulders, and said it all in his ear.

HANSEL AND GRETEL

Hard by a great forest dwelt a poor woodcutter with his wife and his two children. The boy was named Hansel and the girl Gretel. He had little to bite and to break, and once when great scarcity fell on the land, he could no longer procure daily bread.

Now when he thought over this by night in his bed, and tossed about in his anxiety, he groaned and said to his wife, "What is to become of us? How are we to feed our poor children, when we no longer have anything even for ourselves?"

"I'll tell you what, husband," answered the woman, "Early tomorrow morning we will take the children out into the forest to where it is the thickest, there we will light a fire for them, and give each of them one piece of bread more, and then we will go to our work and leave them alone. They will not find the way home again, and we shall be rid of them."

"No, wife," said the man, "I will not do that; how can I bear to leave my children alone in the forest? The wild animals would soon come and tear them to pieces."

"O, thou fool!" said she, "Then we must all four die of hunger; thou mayest as well plane the planks for our coffins," and she left him no peace until he consented.

"But I feel very sorry for the poor children, all the same," said the man.

The two children had also not been able to sleep for hunger, and had heard what their stepmother had said to their father. Gretel wept bitter tears, and said to Hansel, "Now all is over with us." "Be quiet, Gretel," said Hansel, "do not distress thyself, I will soon find a way to help us."

And when the old folks had fallen asleep, he got up, put on his little coat, opened the door below, and crept outside. The moon shone brightly, and the white pebbles which lay in front of the house glittered like real silver pennies. Hansel stooped and put as many of them in the little pocket of his coat as he could possibly get in. Then he went back and said to Gretel, "Be comforted, dear little sister, and sleep in peace, God will not forsake us," and he lay down again in his bed.

When day dawned, but before the sun had risen, the woman came and awoke the two children, saying "Get up, you sluggards! we are going into the forest to fetch wood."

She gave each a little piece of bread, and said, "There is something for your dinner, but do not eat it up before then, for you will get nothing else."

Gretel took the bread under her apron, as Hansel had the stones in his pocket. Then they all set out together on the way to the forest. When they had walked a short time, Hansel stood still and peeped back at the house, and did so again and again. His father said, "Hansel, what art thou looking at there and staying behind for? Mind what thou art about, and do not forget how to use thy legs."

"Ah, father," said Hansel, "I am looking at my little white cat, which is sitting up on the roof, and wants to say good-bye to me."

The wife said, "Fool, that is not thy little cat, that is the morning sun which is shining on the chimneys."

Hansel, however, had not been looking back at the cat, but had been constantly throwing one of the white pebble-stones out of his pocket on the road.

When they had reached the middle of the forest, the father said, "Now, children, pile up some wood, and I will light a fire that you may not be cold." Hansel and Gretel gathered brushwood together, as high as a little hill. The brushwood was lighted, and when the flames were burning very high, the woman said, "Now, children, lay yourselves down by the fire and rest, we will go into the forest and cut some wood. When we have done, we will come back and fetch you away."

*Hansel stooped and put as many of them in the little pocket of his coat
as he could possibly get in*

Hansel and Gretel sat by the fire, and when noon came, each ate a little piece of bread, and as they heard the strokes of the woodax they believed that their father was near. It was not, however, the ax, it was a branch which he had fastened to a withered tree which the wind was blowing backwards and forwards. And as they had been sitting such a long time, their eyes shut with fatigue, and they fell fast asleep.

When at last they awoke, it was already dark night. Gretel began to cry and said, "How are we to get out of the forest now?"

But Hansel comforted her and said, "Just wait a little, until the moon has risen, and then we will soon find the way."

And when the full moon had risen, Hansel took his little sister by the hand, and followed the pebbles which shone like newly-coined silver pieces, and showed them the way. They walked the whole night long, and by break of day came once more to their father's house. They knocked at the door, and when the woman opened it and saw that it was Hansel and Gretel, she said, "You naughty children, why have you slept so long in the forest? We thought you were never coming back at all!" The father, however, rejoiced, for it had cut him to the heart to leave them behind alone.

Not long afterwards, there was once more great scarcity in all parts, and the children heard their mother saying at night to their father, "Everything is eaten again, we have one half loaf left, and after that there is an end. The children must go, we will take them farther into the wood, so that they will not find their way out again; there is no other means of saving ourselves!"

The man's heart was heavy, and he thought "it would be better for thee to share the last mouthful with thy children." The woman, however, would listen to nothing that he had to say, but scolded and reproached him. He who says A must say B, likewise, and as he had yielded the first time, he had to do so a second time also.

The children were, however, still awake and had heard the conversation. When the old folks were asleep, Hansel again got up, and wanted to go out and pick up pebbles as he had done before, but the woman had locked the door, and Hansel could not get out. Nevertheless he comforted his little sister, and said, "Do not cry, Gretel, go to sleep quietly, the good God will help us."

Early in the morning came the woman, and took the children out of their beds. Their bit of bread was given to them, but it was still smaller than the time before. On the way into the forest Hansel crumbled his in his pocket, and often stood still and threw a morsel on the ground.

"Hansel, why dost thou stop and look round?" said the father, "go on."

"I am looking back at my little pigeon which is sitting on the roof, and wants to say good-bye to me," answered Hansel.

"Simpleton!" said the woman, "that is not thy little pigeon, that is the morning sun that is shining on the chimney."

Hansel, however, little by little, threw all the crumbs on the path.

The woman led the children still deeper into the forest, where they had never in their lives been before. Then a great fire was again made, and the mother said, "Just sit there, you children, and when you are tired you may sleep a little; we are going into the forest to cut wood, and in the evening when we are done, we will come and fetch you away."

When it was noon, Gretel shared her piece of bread with Hansel, who had scattered his by the way. Then they fell asleep and evening came and went, but no one came to the poor children. They did not awake until it was dark night, and Hansel comforted his little sister and said, "Just wait, Gretel, until the moon rises, and then we shall see the crumbs of bread which I have strewn about, they will show us our way home again."

When the moon came they set out, but they found no crumbs, for the many thousands of birds which fly about in the woods and fields had picked them all up. Hansel said to Gretel, "We shall soon find the way," but they did not find it. They walked the whole night and all the next day too from morning till evening, but they did not get out of the forest, and were very hungry, for they had nothing to eat but two or three berries, which grew on the ground. And as they were so weary that their legs would carry them no longer, they lay down beneath a tree and fell asleep.

It was now three mornings since they had left their father's house. They began to walk again, but they always got deeper into the forest, and if help did not come soon, they must die of hunger and weariness. When it was mid-day, they saw a beautiful snow-white bird sitting on a bough, which sang so delightfully that they stood still and listened to it. And when it had finished its song, it spread its wings and flew away before them, and they followed it until they reached a little house, on the roof of which it alighted; and when they came quite up to little house they saw that it was built of bread and covered with cakes, but that the windows were of clear sugar.

"We will set to work on that," said Hansel, "and have a good meal. I will eat a bit of the roof, and thou, Gretel, canst eat some of the window, it will taste sweet."

Hansel reached up above, and broke off a little of the roof to try how it tasted, and Gretel leaned against the window and nibbled at the panes. Then a soft voice cried from the room,

> Nibble, nibble, gnaw,
> Who is nibbling at my little house?

The children answered,

> The wind, the wind,
> The heaven-born wind,

and went on eating without disturbing themselves. Hansel, who thought the roof tasted very nice, tore down a great piece of it, and Gretel pushed out the whole of one round windowpane, sat down, and enjoyed herself with it. Suddenly, the door opened, and a very, very old woman, who supported herself on crutches, came creeping out. Hansel and Gretel were so terribly frightened that they let fall what they had in their hands. The old woman, however, nodded her head, and said, "Oh, you dear children, who has brought you here? Do come in, and stay with me. No harm shall happen to you."

She took them both by the hand, and led them into her little house. Then good food was set before them: milk and pancakes, with sugar, apples, and nuts. Afterwards two pretty little beds were covered with clean white linen, and Hansel and Gretel lay down in them, and thought they were in heaven.

The old woman had only pretended to be so kind; she was in reality a wicked witch who lay in wait for children, and who had only built the little house of bread in order to entice them there. When a child fell under her power, she killed, cooked, and ate it, and that was a feast day with her. Witches have red eyes, and cannot see far, but they have a keen scent like the beasts, and are aware when human beings draw near. When Hansel and Gretel came into her neighborhood, she laughed maliciously, and said mockingly, "I have them, they shall not escape me again!"

Suddenly, the door opened, and a very, very old woman,
who supported herself on crutches, came creeping out

Early in the morning before the children were awake, she was already up, and when she saw both of them sleeping and looking so pretty, with their plump red cheeks, she muttered to herself, "That will be a dainty mouthful!"

Then she seized Hansel with her shrivelled hand, carried him into a little stable, and shut him in behind a grated door. He might scream as he liked; it was of no use. Then she went to Gretel, shook her till she awoke, and cried, "Get up, lazy thing, fetch some water, and cook something good for thy brother. He is in the stable outside, and is to be made fat. When he is fat, I will eat him." Gretel began to weep bitterly, but it was all in vain; she was forced to do what the wicked witch ordered her.

And now the best food was cooked for poor Hansel, but Gretel got nothing but crab-shells. Every morning the woman crept to the little stable, and cried, "Hansel, stretch out thy finger that I may feel if thou wilt soon be fat." Hansel, however, stretched out a little bone to her, and the old woman, who had dim eyes, could not see it, and thought it was Hansel's finger, and was astonished that there was no way of fattening him. When four weeks had gone by, and Hansel still continued thin, she was seized with impatience and would not wait any longer.

"Gretel," she cried to the girl, "be active, and bring some water. Let Hansel be fat or lean, tomorrow I will kill him, and cook him."

Ah, how the poor little sister did lament when she had to fetch the water, and how her tears did flow down over her cheeks! "Dear God, do help us," she cried. "If the wild beasts in the forest had but devoured us, we should at any rate have died together."

"Just keep thy noise to thyself," said the old woman, "all that won't help thee at all."

Early in the morning, Gretel had to go out and hang up the cauldron with the water, and light the fire. "We will bake first," said the old woman, "I have already heated the oven, and kneaded the dough."

She pushed poor Gretel out to the oven, from which flames of fire were already darting. "Creep in," said the witch, "and see if it is properly heated, so that we can shut the bread in." And when once Gretel was inside, she intended to shut the oven and let her bake in it, and then she would eat her, too.

But Gretel saw what she had in her mind, and said, "I do not know how I am to do it; how do you get in?"

Hansel, however, stretched out a little bone to her, and the old woman,
who had dim eyes, could not see it, and thought it was Hansel's finger,
and was astonished that there was no way of fattening him

"Silly goose," said the old woman, "The door is big enough; just look, I can get in myself!" and she crept up and thrust her head into the oven.

Then Gretel gave her a push that drove her far into it, and shut the iron door, and fastened the bolt. Oh! then she began to howl quite horribly, but Gretel ran away, and the godless witch was miserably burnt to death.

Gretel, however, ran like lightning to Hansel, opened his little stable, and cried, "Hansel, we are saved! The old witch is dead!" Then Hansel sprang out like a bird from its cage when the door is opened for it. How they did rejoice and embrace each other, and dance about and kiss each other! And as they had no longer any need to fear her, they went into the witch's house, and in every corner there stood chests full of pearls and jewels.

"These are far better than pebbles!" said Hansel, and thrust into his pockets whatever could be got in, and Gretel said, "I, too, will take something home with me," and filled her pinafore full.

"Silly goose," said the old woman, "The door is big enough; just look, I can get in myself!"

"But now we will go away," said Hansel, "that we may get out of the witch's forest."

When they had walked for two hours, they came to a great piece of water. "We cannot get over," said Hansel, "I see no foot-plank, and no bridge." "And no boat crosses either," answered Gretel, "but a white duck is swimming there; if I ask her, she will help us over." Then she cried,

> Little duck, little duck, dost thou see,
> Hansel and Gretel are waiting for thee?
> There's never a plank, or bridge in sight,
> Take us across on thy back so white.

The duck came to them, and Hansel seated himself on its back, and told his sister to sit by him. "No," replied Gretel, "that will be too heavy for the little duck; she shall take us across, one after the other."

The good little duck did so, and when they were once safely across and had walked for a short time, the forest seemed to be more and more familiar to them, and at length they saw from afar their father's house. Then they began to run, rushed into the parlor, and threw themselves into their father's arms. The man had not known one happy hour since he had left the children in the forest; the woman, however, was dead. Gretel emptied her pinafore until pearls and precious stones ran about the room, and Hansel threw one handful after another out of his pocket to add to them. Then all anxiety was at an end, and they lived together in perfect happiness. My tale is done, there runs a mouse, whosoever catches it, may make himself a big fur cap out of it.

❧

THE GOLDEN BIRD

In the olden time there was a king who had behind his palace a beautiful pleasure-garden in which there was a tree that bore golden apples. When the apples were getting ripe they were counted, but on the very next morning one was missing. This was told to the King, and he ordered that a watch should be kept every night beneath the tree.

The King had three sons, the eldest of whom he sent, as soon as night came on, into the garden; but when midnight came he could not keep himself from sleeping, and next morning again an apple was gone.

The following night the second son had to keep watch, and it fared no better with him; as soon as twelve o'clock had struck he fell asleep, and in the morning an apple was gone.

Now it came to the turn of the third son to watch. He was quite ready, but the King had not much trust in him, and thought that he would be of less use even than his brothers; but at last he let him go. The youth lay down beneath the tree, but kept awake, and did not let sleep master him. When it struck twelve, something rustled through the air, and in the moonlight he saw a bird coming whose feathers were all shining with gold. The bird alighted on the tree, and had just plucked off an apple, when the youth shot an arrow at him. The bird flew off, but the arrow had struck his plumage, and one of his golden feathers fell down. The youth picked it up, and the next morning took it to the King and told him what he had seen in the night.

The King called his council together, and everyone declared that a feather like this was worth more than the whole kingdom. "If the feather is so precious," declared the King, "one alone will not do for me; I must and will have the whole bird!"

The eldest son set out; he trusted to his cleverness, and thought that he would easily find the Golden Bird. When he had gone some distance he saw a Fox sitting at the edge of a wood, so he cocked his gun and took aim at him.

The Fox cried, "Do not shoot me! and in return I will give you some good counsel. You are on the way to the Golden Bird; and this evening you will come to a village in which stand two inns opposite to one another. One of them is lighted up brightly, and all goes on merrily within, but do not go into it; go rather into the other, even though it seems a bad one."

"How can such a silly beast give wise advice?" thought the King's son, and he pulled the trigger. But he missed the Fox, who stretched out his tail and ran quickly into the wood.

So he pursued his way, and by evening came to the village where the two inns were; in one they were singing and dancing; the other had a poor, miserable look. "I should be a fool, indeed," he thought, "if I were to go into the shabby tavern, and pass by the good one." So he went into the cheerful one, lived there in riot and revel, and forgot the bird and his father, and all good counsels.

When some time had passed, and the eldest son for month after month did not come back home, the second set out, wishing to find the Golden Bird. The Fox met him as he had met the eldest, and gave him the good advice of which he took no heed. He came to the two inns, and his brother was standing at the window of the one from which came the music, and called out to him. He could not resist, but went inside and lived only for pleasure.

Again some time passed, and then the King's youngest son wanted to set off and try his luck, but his father would not allow it. "It is of no use," said he, "he will find the Golden Bird still less than his brothers, and if a mishap were to befall him he knows not how to help himself; he is a little wanting at the best." But at last, as he had no peace, he let him go.

Again the Fox was sitting outside the wood, and begged for his life, and offered his good advice. The youth was good-natured, and said, "Be easy, little Fox, I will do you no harm." "You shall not repent it," answered the Fox; "and that you may get on more quickly, get up behind on my tail." And scarcely had he seated himself when the Fox began to run, and away he went over stock and stone till his hair whistled in the wind. When they came to the village the youth got off; he followed the good advice, and without looking round turned into the little inn, where he spent the night quietly.

The next morning, as soon as he got into the open country, there sat the Fox already, and said, "I will tell you further what you have to do. Go on quite straight, and at last you will come to a castle, in front of which a whole regiment of soldiers is lying, but do not trouble yourself about them, for they will all be asleep and snoring. Go through the midst of them straight into the castle, and go through all the rooms, till at last you will come to a chamber where a Golden Bird is hanging in a wooden cage. Close by, there stands an empty gold cage for show, but beware of taking the bird out of the common cage and putting it into the fine one, or it may go badly with you." With these words the Fox again stretched out his tail, and the King's son seated himself upon it, and away he went over stock and stone till his hair whistled in the wind.

When he came to the castle he found everything as the Fox had said. The King's son went into the chamber where the Golden Bird was shut up

Away he went over stock and stone till his hair whistled in the wind

in a wooden cage, whilst a golden one stood hard by; and the three golden apples lay about the room. "But," thought he, "it would be absurd if I were to leave the beautiful bird in the common and ugly cage," so he opened the door, laid hold of it, and put it into the golden cage. But at the same moment the bird uttered a shrill cry. The soldiers awoke, rushed in, and took him off to prison. The next morning he was taken before a court of justice, and as he confessed everything, was sentenced to death.

The King, however, said that he would grant him his life on one condition: namely, if he brought him the Golden Horse which ran faster than the wind; and in that case he should receive, over and above, as a reward, the Golden Bird.

The King's son set off, but he sighed and was sorrowful, for how was he to find the Golden Horse? But all at once he saw his old friend the Fox sitting on the road. "Look you," said the Fox, "this has happened because you did not give heed to me. However, be of good courage. I will give you my help, and tell you how to get to the Golden Horse. You must go straight on, and you will come to a castle, where in the stable stands the horse. The grooms will be lying in front of the stable; but they will be asleep and snoring, and you can quietly lead out the Golden Horse. But of one thing you must take heed; put on him the common saddle of wood and leather, and not the golden one, which hangs close by, else it will go ill with you." Then the Fox stretched out his tail, the King's son seated himself upon it, and away he went over stock and stone until his hair whistled in the wind.

Everything happened just as the Fox had said; the prince came to the stable in which the Golden Horse was standing, but just as he was going to put the common saddle upon him, he thought, "It will be a shame to such a beautiful beast, if I do not give him the good saddle which belongs to him by right." But scarcely had the golden saddle touched the horse than he began to neigh loudly. The grooms awoke, seized the youth, and threw him into prison. The next morning he was sentenced by the court to death; but the King promised to grant him his life, and the Golden Horse as well, if he could bring back the beautiful princess from the Golden Castle.

With a heavy heart the youth set out; yet luckily for him he soon found the trusty Fox. "I ought only to leave you to your ill-luck," said the Fox, "but I pity you, and will help you once more out of your trouble. This road takes you straight to the Golden Castle, you will reach it by eventide; and at night when everything is quiet the beautiful princess goes to the bathing-house to bathe. When she enters it, run up to her and give her a kiss, then she will follow you, and you can take her away with you; only do not allow her to take leave of her parents first, or it will go ill with you."

Then the Fox stretched out his tail, the King's son seated himself upon it, and away the Fox went, over stock and stone, till his hair whistled in the wind.

When he reached the Golden Castle it was just as the Fox had said. He waited until midnight, when everything lay in deep sleep, and the beautiful princess was going to the bathing-house. Then he sprang out and gave her a kiss. She said that she would like to go with him, but she asked him pitifully, and with tears, to allow her first to take leave of her parents. At first he withstood her prayer, but when she wept more and more, and fell at his feet, he at last gave in. But no sooner had the maiden reached the bedside of her father than he and all the rest in the castle awoke, and the youth was laid hold of and put into prison.

The next morning the King said to him, "Your life is forfeited, and you can only find mercy if you take away the hill which stands in front of my windows, and prevents my seeing beyond it; and you must finish it all within eight days. If you do that you shall have my daughter as your reward."

The King's son began, and dug and shoveled without leaving off, but when after seven days he saw how little he had done, and how all his work was as good as nothing, he fell into great sorrow and gave up all hope. But on the evening of the seventh day the Fox appeared and said, "You do not deserve that I should take any trouble about you; but just go away and lie down to sleep, and I will do the work for you."

The next morning when he awoke and looked out of the window the hill had gone. The youth ran, full of joy, to the King, and told him that the task was fulfilled, and whether he liked it or not, the King had to hold to his word and give him his daughter.

So the two set forth together, and it was not long before the trusty Fox came up with them. "You have certainly got what is best," said he, "but the Golden Horse also belongs to the maiden of the Golden Castle."

"How shall I get it?" asked the youth.

"That I will tell you," answered the Fox. "First take the beautiful maiden to the King who sent you to the Golden Castle. There will be unheard-of rejoicing; they will gladly give you the Golden Horse, and will bring it out to you. Mount it as soon as possible, and offer your hand to all in farewell; last of all to the beautiful maiden. And as soon as you have taken her hand swing her up on to the horse, and gallop away, and no one will be able to bring you back, for the horse runs faster than the wind."

The King's son carried off the beautiful princess on the Golden Horse

All was carried out successfully, and the King's son carried off the beautiful princess on the Golden Horse.

The Fox did not remain behind, and he said to the youth, "Now I will help you to get the Golden Bird. When you come near to the castle where the Golden Bird is to be found, let the maiden get down, and I will take her into my care. Then ride with the Golden Horse into the castle-yard; there will be great rejoicing at the sight, and they will bring out the Golden Bird for you. As soon as you have the cage in your hand gallop back to us, and take the maiden away again."

When the plan had succeeded, and the King's son was about to ride home with his treasures, the Fox said, "Now you shall reward me for my help."

"What do you require for it?" asked the youth.

"When you get into the wood yonder, shoot me dead, and chop off my head and feet."

"That would be fine gratitude," said the King's son. "I cannot possibly do that for you."

The Fox said, "If you will not do it I must leave you, but before I go away I will give you a piece of good advice. Be careful about two things. Buy no gallows'-flesh, and do not sit at the edge of any well." And then he ran into the wood.

The youth thought, "That is a wonderful beast, he has strange whims; who is going to buy gallows'-flesh? And the desire to sit at the edge of a well it has never yet seized me."

He rode on with the beautiful maiden, and his road took him again through the village in which his two brothers had remained. There was a great stir and noise, and, when he asked what was going on, he was told that two men were going to be hanged. As he came nearer to the place he saw that they were his brothers, who had been playing all kinds of wicked pranks, and had squandered all their wealth. He inquired whether they could not be set free.

"If you will pay for them," answered the people; "but why should you waste your money on wicked men, and buy them free." He did not think twice about it, but paid for them, and when they were set free they all went on their way together.

They came to the wood where the Fox had first met them, as it was cool and pleasant within it, the two brothers said, "Let us rest a little by the well, and eat and drink." He agreed, and whilst they were talking he forgot himself, and sat down upon the edge of the well without thinking of any evil. But the two brothers threw him backwards into the well, took the maiden, the Horse, and the Bird, and went home to their father. "Here we bring you not only the Golden Bird," said they; "we have won the Golden Horse also, and the maiden from the Golden Castle." Then was there great joy; but the Horse would not eat, the Bird would not sing, and the maiden sat and wept.

But the youngest brother was not dead. By good fortune the well was dry, and he fell upon soft moss without being hurt; but he could not get out again. Even in this strait the faithful Fox did not leave him: it came and leapt down to him, and upbraided him for having forgotten its advice. "But yet I cannot give it up so," he said; "I will help you up again into daylight." He bade him grasp his tail and keep tight hold of it; and then he pulled him up.

"You are not out of all danger yet," said the Fox. "Your brothers were not sure of your death, and have surrounded the wood with watchers, who are to kill you if you let yourself be seen." But a poor man was sitting upon the road, with whom the youth changed clothes, and in this way he got to the King's palace.

No one knew him, but the Bird began to sing, the Horse began to eat, and the beautiful maiden left off weeping. The King, astonished, asked, "What does this mean?" Then the maiden said, "I do not know, but I have been so sorrowful and now I am so happy! I feel as if my true bridegroom had come." She told him all that had happened, although the other brothers had threatened her with death if she were to betray anything.

The King commanded that all people who were in his castle should be brought before him; and amongst them came the youth in his ragged clothes; but the maiden knew him at once and fell upon his neck. The wicked brothers were seized and put to death, but he was married to the beautiful maiden and declared heir to the King.

But how did it fare with the poor Fox? Long afterwards the King's son was once again walking in the wood, when the Fox met him and said, "You have everything now that you can wish for, but there is never an end to my misery, and yet it is in your power to free me," and again he asked him with tears to shoot him dead and chop off his head and feet. So he did it, and scarcely was it done when the Fox was changed into a man, and was no other than the brother of the beautiful princess, who at last was freed from the magic charm which had been laid upon him.

And now nothing more was wanting to their happiness as long as they lived.

⸏⸏

THE RAVEN

There was once upon a time a Queen who had a little daughter who was still so young that she had to be carried. One day the child was naughty, and the mother might say what she liked, but the child would not be quiet. Then she became impatient, and as the ravens were flying about the palace, she opened the window and said, "I wish you were a raven and would fly away, and then I should have some rest." Scarcely had she spoken the words, before the child was changed into a raven, and flew from her arms out of the window. It flew into a dark forest, and stayed in it a long time, and the parents heard nothing of their child.

Then one day a man was on his way through this forest and heard the raven crying, and followed the voice, and when he came nearer, the bird said, "I am a king's daughter by birth, and am bewitched, but thou canst set me free."

"What am I to do," asked he.

She said, "Go further into the forest, and thou wilt find a house, wherein sits an aged woman, who will offer thee meat and drink, but you must accept nothing, for if thou eatest and drinkest anything, thou wilt fall into a sleep, and then thou wilt not be able to deliver me. In the garden behind the house there is a great heap of tan, and on this thou shalt stand and wait for me. For three days I will come every afternoon at two o'clock in a carriage. On the first day four white horses will be harnessed to it, then four chestnut horses, and lastly four black ones; but if thou art not awake, but sleeping, I shall not be set free."

The man promised to do everything that she desired, but the raven said, alas, "I know already that thou wilt not deliver me; thou wilt accept something from the woman."

Then the man once more promised that he would certainly not touch anything either to eat or to drink. But when he entered the house the old woman came to him and said, "Poor man, how faint you are; come and refresh yourself; eat and drink."

"No," said the man, "I will not eat or drink."

She, however, let him have no peace, and said, "If you will not eat, take one drink out of the glass; one is nothing."

Then he let himself be persuaded, and drank. Shortly before two o'clock in the afternoon he went into the garden to the tan heap to wait for the raven. As he was standing there, his weariness all at once became so great that he could not struggle against it, and lay down for a short time, but he was determined not to go to sleep. Hardly, however, had he lain down, than his eyes closed of their own accord, and he fell asleep and slept so soundly that nothing in the world could have aroused him.

At two o'clock the raven came driving up with four white horses, but she was already in deep grief and said, "I know he is asleep." And when she came into the garden, he was indeed lying there asleep on the heap of tan. She alighted from the carriage, went to him, shook him, and called him, but he did not awake.

Next day about noon, the old woman came again and brought him food and drink, but he would not take any of it. But she let him have no rest and persuaded him until at length he again took one drink out of the glass. Towards two o'clock he went into the garden to the tan heap to wait for the raven, but all at once felt such a great weariness that his limbs would no longer support him. He could not help himself, and was forced to lie down, and fell into a heavy sleep. When the raven drove up with four brown horses, she was already full of grief, and said, "I know he is asleep." She went to him, but there he lay sleeping, and there was no wakening him.

Next day the old woman asked what was the meaning of this? He was neither eating nor drinking anything; did he want to die? He replied, "I am not allowed to eat or drink, and will not do so." But she set a dish with food, and a glass with wine before him, and when he smelt it he could not resist, and swallowed a deep draught. When the time came, he went out into the garden to the heap of tan, and waited for the King's daughter; but he became still more weary than on the day before, and lay down and slept as soundly as if he had been a stone.

At two o'clock the raven came with four black horses, and the coachman and everything else was black. She was already in the deepest grief, and said, "I know that he is asleep and cannot deliver me." When she came to him, there he was lying fast asleep. She shook him and called him, but she could not waken him. Then she laid a loaf beside him, and after that a piece of meat, and thirdly a bottle of wine, and he might consume as much of all of them as he liked, but they would never grow less. After this she took a gold ring from her finger, and put it on his, and her name was graven on it. Lastly, she laid a letter beside him wherein was written what she had given him, and that none of the things would ever grow less; and in it was also written, "I see right well that here thou will never be able to deliver me, but if thou art still willing to deliver me, come to the golden castle of Stromberg; it lies in thy power, of that I am certain." And when she had given him all these things, she seated herself in her carriage, and drove to the golden castle of Stromberg.

When the man awoke and saw that he had slept, he was sad at heart, and said, "She has certainly driven by, and I have not set her free." Then he perceived the things which were lying beside him, and read the letter wherein was written how everything had happened. So he arose and went away, intending to go to the golden castle of Stromberg, but he did not know where it was. After he had walked about the world for a long time, he entered into a dark forest, and walked for fourteen days, and still could not find his way out. Then it was once more evening, and he was so tired that he lay down in a thicket and fell asleep. Next day he went onwards, and in the evening, as he was again about to lie down beneath some bushes, he heard such a howling and crying that he could not go to sleep. And at the time when people light the candles, he saw one glimmering, and arose and went towards it. Then he came to a house which seemed very small, for in front of it a great giant was standing. He thought to himself, "If I go in, and the giant sees me, it will very likely cost me my life."

At length he ventured it and went in. When the giant saw him, he said, "It is well that thou comest, for it is long since I have eaten; I will at once eat thee for my supper."

"I'd rather you would leave that alone," said the man, "I do not like to be eaten; but if thou hast any desire to eat, I have quite enough here to satisfy thee."

"If that be true," said the giant, "thou mayst be easy, I was only going to devour thee because I had nothing else."

Then they went, and sat down to the table, and the man took out the bread, wine, and meat which would never come to an end. "This pleases me well," said the giant, and ate to his heart's content.

Then the man said to him, "Canst thou tell me where the golden castle of Stromberg is?"

The giant said, "I will look at my map; all the towns, and villages, and houses are to be found on it." He brought out the map which he had in the room and looked for the castle, but it was not to be found on it. "It's no matter!" said he, "I have some still larger maps in my cupboard upstairs, and we will look in them." But there, too, it was in vain.

The man now wanted to go onwards, but the giant begged him to wait a few days longer until his brother, who had gone out to bring some provisions, came home. When the brother came home they inquired about the golden castle of Stromberg. He replied, "When I have eaten and have had enough, I will look in the map." Then he went with them up to his chamber, and they searched in his map, but could not find it. Then he brought out still older

The golden castle of Stromberg

maps, and they never rested until they found the golden castle of Stromberg, but it was many thousand miles away.

"How am I to get there?" asked the man.

The giant said, "I have two hours' time, during which I will carry you into the neighborhood, but after that I must be at home to suckle the child that we have."

So the giant carried the man to about a hundred leagues from the castle, and said, "Thou canst very well walk the rest of the way alone." And he turned back, but the man went onwards day and night, until at length he came to the golden castle of Stromberg. It stood on a glass-mountain, and the bewitched maiden drove in her carriage round the castle, and then went inside it. He rejoiced when he saw her and wanted to climb up to her, but when he began to do so he always slipped down the glass again. And when he saw that he could not reach her, he was filled with trouble, and said to himself, "I will stay down here below, and wait for her."

So he built himself a hut and stayed in it for a whole year, and every day saw the King's daughter driving about above, but never could go to her. Then one day he saw from his hut three robbers who were beating each other, and cried to them, "God be with ye!" They stopped when they heard the cry, but as they saw no one, they once more began to beat each other, and that too most dangerously. So he again cried, "God be with ye!" Again they stopped, looked round about, but as they saw no one they went on beating each other. Then he cried for the third time, "God be with ye," and thought, "I must see what these three are about," and went thither and asked why they were beating each other so furiously. One of them said that he found a stick, and that when he struck a door with it, that door would spring open. The next said that he had found a mantle, and that whenever he put it on, he was invisible, but the third said he had found a horse on which a man could ride everywhere, even up the glass-mountain. And now they did not know whether they ought to have these things in common, or whether they ought to divide them.

Then the man said, "I will give you something in exchange for these three things. Money indeed have I not, but I have other things of more value; but first I must try yours to see if you have told the truth." Then they put him on the horse, threw the mantle round him, and gave him the stick in his hand, and when he had all these things they were no longer able to see him. So he

*One day he saw from his hut three robbers
who were beating each other*

gave them some vigorous blows and cried, "Now, vagabonds, you have got
what you deserve, are you satisfied?"

And he rode up the glass-mountain, but when he came in front of the
castle at the top, it was shut. Then he struck the door with his stick, and it
sprang open immediately. He went in and ascended the stairs until he came
to the hall where the maiden was sitting with a golden cup full of wine before
her. She, however, could not see him because he had the mantle on. And
when he came up to her, he drew from his finger the ring which she had given
him, and threw it into the cup so that it rang. Then she cried, "That is my
ring, so the man who is to set me free must be here." They searched the whole
castle and did not find him, but he had gone out, and had seated himself on
the horse and thrown off the mantle. When they came to the door, they saw
him and cried aloud in their delight. Then he alighted and took the King's
daughter in his arms, but she kissed him and said, "Now hast thou set me
free, and tomorrow we will celebrate our wedding."

THE KING OF THE GOLDEN MOUNTAIN

There was a certain merchant who had two children, a boy and a girl; they were both young, and could not walk. And two richly-laden ships of his sailed forth to sea with all his property on board, and just as he was expecting to win much money by them, news came that they had gone to the bottom, and now instead of being a rich man he was a poor one, and had nothing left but one field outside the town.

In order to drive his misfortune a little out of his thoughts, he went out to this field, and as he was walking forwards and backwards in it, a little black mannikin stood suddenly by his side, and asked why he was so sad, and what he was taking so much to heart.

Then said the merchant, "If thou couldst help me I would willingly tell thee."

"Who knows?" replied the black dwarf. "Perhaps, I can help thee."

Then the merchant told him that all he possessed had gone to the bottom of the sea, and that he had nothing left but this field.

"Do not trouble thyself," said the dwarf. "If thou wilt promise to give me the first thing that rubs itself against thy leg when thou art at home again, and to bring it here to this place in twelve years' time, thou shalt have as much money as thou wilt."

The merchant thought, "What can that be but my dog?" and did not remember his little boy, so he said yes, gave the black man a written and sealed promise, and went home.

When he reached home, his little boy was so delighted that he held by a bench, tottered up to him, and seized him fast by the legs. The father was shocked, for he remembered his promise, and now knew what he had pledged himself to do. As he still found no money in his chest, he thought the dwarf had only been jesting. But a month afterwards, when he went up to the garret intending to gather together some old tin to sell, he saw a great heap of money lying there. Then he was happy again, made purchases, became a greater merchant than before, and felt that this world was well-governed.

In the meantime the boy grew tall, and at the same time sharp and clever. But the nearer the twelfth year approached the more anxious grew the merchant, so that his distress might be seen in his face. One day his son asked what ailed him, but the father would not say. The boy, however, persisted so long, that at last he told him that without being aware of what he was doing, he had promised him to a black dwarf, and had received much money for doing so. He said likewise that he had set his hand and seal to this, and that now when twelve years had gone by he would have to give him up.

Then said the son, "Oh, father, do not be uneasy, all will go well. The black man has no power over me." The son had himself been blessed by the priest, and when the time came, father and son went together to the field, and the son made a circle and placed himself inside it with his father.

Then came the black dwarf and said to the old man, "Hast thou brought with thee that which thou hast promised me?"

He was silent, but the son asked, "What dost thou want here?"

Then said the black dwarf, "I have to speak with thy father, and not with thee."

The son replied, "Thou hast betrayed and misled my father, give back the writing."

"No," said the black dwarf, "I will not give up my rights."

They spoke together for a long time after this, but at last they agreed that the son, as he did not belong to the enemy of mankind, nor yet to his father, should seat himself in a small boat, which should lie on water which was flowing away from them, and that the father should push it off with his own foot, and then the son should remain given up to the water. So he took leave of his father, placed himself in a little boat, and the father had to push it off with his own foot. The boat capsized so that the keel was uppermost, and the father believed his son was lost, and went home and mourned for him.

The boat, however, did not sink, but floated quietly away, and the boy sat safely inside it, and it floated thus for a long time, until at last it stopped by an unknown shore. Then he landed and saw a beautiful castle before him, and set out to go to it.

But when he entered it, he found that it was bewitched. He went through every room, but all were empty until he reached the last, where a snake lay coiled in a ring. The snake, however, was an enchanted maiden, who rejoiced to see him, and said, "Hast thou come, oh, my deliverer? I have

. . . and the son made a circle and placed himself inside it with his father

already waited twelve years for thee; this kingdom is bewitched, and thou must set it free."

"How can I do that?" he inquired.

"Tonight come twelve black men, covered with chains who will ask what thou art doing here; keep silent; give them no answer, and let them do what they will with thee; they will torment thee, beat thee, stab thee; let everything pass, only do not speak; at twelve o'clock, they must go away again. On the second night twelve others will come; on the third, four-and-twenty, who will cut off thy head, but at twelve o'clock their power will be over, and then if thou hast endured all, and hast not spoken the slightest word, I shall be released. I will come to thee, and will have, in a bottle, some of the water of life. I will rub thee with that, and then thou wilt come to life again, and be as healthy as before."

Then said he, "I will gladly set thee free."

And everything happened just as she had said; the black men could not force a single word from him, and on the third night the snake became a beautiful princess, who came with the water of life and brought him back to life again. So she threw herself into his arms and kissed him, and there was joy and gladness in the whole castle. After this their marriage was celebrated, and he was King of the Golden Mountain.

They lived very happily together, and the Queen bore a fine boy. Eight years had already gone by, when the King bethought him of his father; his heart was moved, and he wished to visit him. The Queen, however, would not let him go away, and said, "I know beforehand that it will cause my unhappiness"; but he suffered her to have no rest until she consented. At their parting she gave him a wishing-ring, and said, "Take this ring and put it on thy finger, and then thou wilt immediately be transported whithersoever thou wouldst be, only thou must promise me not to use it in wishing me away from this place and with thy father." That he promised her, put the ring on his finger, and wished himself at home, just outside the town where his father lived.

Instantly he found himself there, and made for the town, but when he came to the gate, the sentries would not let him in, because he wore such strange and yet such rich and magnificent clothing. Then he went to a hill where a shepherd was watching his sheep, changed clothes with him, put on his old shepherd's-coat, and then entered the town without hindrance.

When he came to his father, he made himself known to him, but he did not at all believe that the shepherd was his son, and said he certainly had had a son, but that he was dead long ago; however, as he saw he was a poor, needy shepherd, he would give him something to eat.

Then the shepherd said to his parents, "I am verily your son. Do you know of no mark on my body by which you could recognize me?"

"Yes," said his mother, "our son had a raspberry mark under his right arm." He slipped back his shirt, and they saw the raspberry under his right arm, and no longer doubted that he was their son. Then he told them that he was King of the Golden Mountain, and a king's daughter was his wife, and that they had a fine son of seven years old.

Then said the father, "That is certainly not true; it is a fine kind of a king who goes about in a ragged shepherd's-coat."

On this the son fell in a passion, and without thinking of his promise, turned his ring round, and wished both his wife and child with him. They were there in a second, but the Queen wept, and reproached him, and said that he had broken his word, and had brought misfortune upon her. He said, "I have done it thoughtlessly, and not with evil intention," and tried to calm her, and she pretended to believe this; but she had mischief in her mind.

Then he led her out of the town into the field, and showed her the stream where the little boat had been pushed off, and then he said, "I am tired; sit down, I will sleep awhile on thy lap." And he laid his head on her lap, and fell asleep. When he was asleep, she first drew the ring from his finger, then she drew away the foot which was under him, leaving only the slipper behind her, and she took her child in her arms, and wished herself back in her own kingdom. When he awoke, there he lay quite deserted, and his wife and child were gone, and so was the ring from his finger, the slipper only was still there as a token. "Home to thy parents thou canst not return," thought he. "They would say that thou wast a wizard; thou must be off, and walk on until thou arrivest in thine own kingdom." So he went away and came at length to a hill by which three giants were standing, disputing with each other because they did not know how to divide their father's property. When they saw him passing by, they called to him and said little men had quick wits, and that he was to divide their inheritance for them.

The inheritance, however, consisted of a sword, which had this property: if any one took it in his hand, and said, "All heads off but mine," every head would lie on the ground; secondly, of a cloak which made anyone who put it on invisible; thirdly, of a pair of boots which could transport the wearer to any place he wished in a moment.

He said, "Give me the three things that I may see if they are still in good condition." They gave him the cloak, and when he had put it on, he was invisible and changed into a fly. Then he resumed his own form and said, "The cloak is a good one, now give me the sword."

They said, "No, we will not give thee that; if thou were to say, 'All heads off but mine,' all our heads would be off, and thou alone wouldst be left with thine." Nevertheless they gave it to him with the condition that he was only to try it against a tree. This he did, and the sword cut in two the trunk of a tree as if it had been a blade of straw.

Then he wanted to have the boots likewise, but they said, "No, we will not give them; if thou hadst them on thy feet and wert to wish thyself at the top of the hill, we should be left down here with nothing."

"Oh, no," said he, "I will not do that." So they gave him the boots as well.

And now when he had got all these things, he thought of nothing but his wife and his child, and said as though to himself, "Oh, if I were but on the Golden Mountain," and at the same moment he vanished from the sight of the giants, and thus their inheritance was divided.

When he was near his palace, he heard sounds of joy, and fiddles, and flutes, and the people told him that his wife was celebrating her wedding with another. Then he fell into a rage, and said, "False woman, she betrayed and deserted me whilst I was asleep!" So he put on his cloak, and unseen by all went into the palace.

When he entered the dining-hall a great table was spread with delicious food, and the guests were eating and drinking, and laughing, and jesting. She sat on a royal seat in the midst of them in splendid apparel, with a crown on her head. He placed himself behind her, and no one saw him. When she put a piece of meat on a plate for herself, he took it away and ate it, and when she poured out a glass of wine for herself, he took it away and drank it. She was always helping herself to something, and yet she never got anything, for plate and glass disappeared immediately.

Then dismayed and ashamed, she arose and went to her chamber and wept, but he followed her there. She said, "Has the devil power over me, or did my deliverer never come?"

Then he struck her in the face, and said, "Did thy deliverer never come? It is he who has thee in his power, thou traitor. Have I deserved this from thee?" Then he made himself visible, went into the hall, and cried, "The wedding is at an end, the true King has returned."

The kings, princes, and councilors who were assembled there, ridiculed and mocked him, but he did not trouble to answer them, and said, "Will you go away, or not?" On this they tried to seize him and pressed upon him, but he drew his sword and said, "All heads off but mine," and all the heads rolled on the ground, and he alone was master, and once more King of the Golden Mountain.

THE SINGING, SOARING LARK

Once upon a time a man was about to set out on a long journey, and on parting he asked his three daughters what he should bring back with him for them. The eldest wished for pearls, the second wished for diamonds, but the third said, "Dear father, I should like a singing, soaring lark."

The father said, "Yes, if I can get it, you shall have it," kissed all three, and set out.

Now when the time had come for him to be on his way home again, he had brought pearls and diamonds for the two eldest, but he had sought everywhere in vain for a singing, soaring lark for the youngest, and he was very unhappy about it, for she was his favorite child. Then his road lay through a forest, and in the midst of it was a splendid castle, and near the castle stood a tree, but quite on the top of the tree, he saw a singing, soaring lark. "Aha, you come just at the right moment!" he said, quite delighted, and called to his servant to climb up and catch the little creature.

But as he approached the tree, a lion leapt from beneath it, shook himself, and roared till the leaves on the trees trembled. "He who tries to steal my singing, soaring lark," he cried, "will I devour."

Then the man said, "I did not know that the bird belonged to thee. I will make amends for the wrong I have done and ransom myself with a large sum of money, only spare my life."

The lion said, "Nothing can save thee, unless thou wilt promise to give me for mine own what first meets thee on thy return home; and if thou wilt do that, I will grant thee thy life, and thou shalt have the bird for thy daughter, into the bargain."

But the man hesitated and said, "That might be my youngest daughter, she loves me best, and always runs to meet me on my return home."

The servant, however, was terrified and said, "Why should your daughter be the very one to meet you, it might as easily be a cat, or dog?" So the man allowed himself to be persuaded, took the singing, soaring lark, and promised to give the lion whatsoever should first meet him on his return home.

When he reached home and entered his house, the first who met him was no other than his youngest and dearest daughter, who came running up, kissed and embraced him, and when she saw that he had brought with him a singing, soaring lark, she was beside herself with joy. The father, however, could not rejoice, but began to weep, and said, "My dearest child, I have bought the little bird dear. In return for it, I have been obliged to promise thee to a savage lion, and when he has thee he will tear thee in pieces and devour thee," and he told her all, just as it had happened, and begged her not to go there, come what might.

But she consoled him and said, "Dearest father, indeed your promise must be fulfilled. I will go thither and soften the lion, so that I may return to thee safely."

Next morning she had the road pointed out to her, took leave, and went fearlessly out into the forest. The lion, however, was an enchanted prince and was by day a lion, and all his people were lions with him, but in the night they resumed their natural human shapes. On her arrival she was kindly received and led into the castle. When night came, the lion turned into a handsome man, and their wedding was celebrated with great magnificence. They lived happily together, remained awake at night, and slept in the daytime.

One day he came and said, "Tomorrow there is a feast in thy father's house, because your eldest sister is to be married, and if thou art inclined to go there, my lions shall conduct thee."

She said, "Yes, I should very much like to see my father again," and went thither, accompanied by the lions. There was great joy when she arrived, for they had all believed that she had been torn in pieces by the lion, and had long ceased to live. But she told them what a handsome husband she had, and how well off she was, remained with them while the wedding-feast lasted, and then went back again to the forest.

When the second daughter was about to be married, and she was again invited to the wedding, she said to the lion, "This time I will not be alone, thou must come with me." The lion, however, said that it was too dangerous for him, for if when there a ray from a burning candle fell on him, he would be changed into a dove, and for seven years long would have to fly about with the doves. She said, "Ah, but do come with me, I will take great care of thee, and guard thee from all light." So they went away together, and took with them their little child as well. She had a chamber built there, so strong and thick that no ray could pierce through it; in this he was to shut himself up when the candles were lit for the wedding-feast. But the door was made of green wood which warped and left a little crack which no one noticed.

. . . and went thither, accompanied by the lions

The wedding was celebrated with magnificence, but when the procession with all its candles and torches came back from church, and passed by this apartment, a ray about the breadth of a hair fell on the King's son, and when this ray touched him, he was transformed in an instant, and when she came in and looked for him, she did not see him, but a white dove was sitting there. The dove said to her, "For seven years must I fly about the world, but at every seventh step that you take I will let fall a drop of red blood and a white feather, and these will show thee the way; and if thou followest the trace thou canst release me." Thereupon the dove flew out at the door, and she followed him, and at every seventh step a red drop of blood and a little white feather fell down and showed her the way.

So she went continually further and further in the wide world, never looking about her or resting, and the seven years were almost past; then she rejoiced and thought that they would soon be delivered, and yet they were so far from it! Once when they were thus moving onwards, no little feather and no drop of red blood fell, and when she raised her eyes the dove had disappeared. And as she thought to herself, "In this no man can help thee," she climbed up to the sun, and said to him, "Thou shinest into every crevice, and over every peak—hast thou not seen a white dove flying?"

"No," said the sun, "I have seen none, but I present thee with a casket; open it when thou art in sorest need."

Then she thanked the sun, and went on until evening came and the moon appeared; she then asked her, "Thou shinest the whole night through, and on every field and forest, hast thou not seen a white dove flying?"

"No," said the moon, "I have seen no dove, but here I give thee an egg, break it when thou art in great need."

She thanked the moon, and went on until the night wind came up and blew on her, then she said to it, "Thou blowest over every tree and under every leaf, hast thou not seen a white dove flying?"

"No," said the night wind, "I have seen none, but I will ask the three other winds, perhaps they have seen it."

The east wind and the west wind came, and had seen nothing, but the south wind said, "I have seen the white dove. It has flown to the Red Sea, where it has become a lion again, for the seven years are over, and the lion is there fighting with a dragon. The dragon, however, is an enchanted princess."

The night wind then said to her, "I will advise thee; go to the Red Sea, on the right bank are some tall reeds, count them, break off the eleventh, and strike the dragon with it, then the lion will be able to subdue it, and both then will regain their human form. After that, look round and thou wilt see the griffin which is by the Red Sea; swing thyself, with thy beloved, on to his back, and the bird will carry you over the sea to your own home. Here is a nut for thee, when thou are above the center of the sea, let the nut fall. It will immediately shoot up, and a tall nut-tree will grow out of the water on which the griffin may rest; for if he cannot rest, he will not be strong enough to carry you across; and if thou forgettest to throw down the nut, he will let you fall into the sea."

Then she went thither, and found everything as the night wind had said. She counted the reeds by the sea, and cut off the eleventh, struck the dragon therewith, whereupon the lion overcame it, and immediately both of them regained their human shapes. But when the princess who had before been the dragon was delivered from enchantment, she took the youth by the arm, seated herself on the griffin, and carried him off with her.

There stood the poor maiden who had wandered so far and was again forsaken. She sat down and cried, but at last she took courage and said, "Still I will go as far as the wind blows and as long as the cock crows, until I find him," and she went forth by long, long roads, until at last she came to the castle where both of them were living together. There she heard that soon a feast was to be held in which they would celebrate their wedding, but she said, "God still helps me," and opened the casket that the sun had given her. A dress lay therein as brilliant as the sun itself. So she took it out and put it on, and went up into the castle, and everyone, even the bride herself, looked at her with astonishment.

The dress pleased the bride so well that she thought it might do for her wedding-dress, and asked if it was for sale? "Not for money or land," answered she, "but for flesh and blood." The bride asked her what she meant by that, so she said, "Let me sleep a night in the chamber where the bridegroom sleeps." The bride would not, yet wanted very much to have the dress; at last she consented, but the page was to give the prince a sleeping-draught.

When it was night, therefore, and the youth was already asleep, she was led into the chamber. She seated herself on the bed and said, "I have followed after thee for seven years. I have been to the sun and the moon, and the four winds, and have inquired for thee, and have helped thee against the dragon; wilt thou, then quite forget me?" But the prince slept so soundly that it only seemed to him as if the wind were whistling outside in the fir-trees.

When therefore day broke, she was led out again, and had to give up the golden dress. And as that even had been of no avail, she was sad, went out into a meadow, sat down there, and wept. While she was sitting there, she thought of the egg which the moon had given her; she opened it, and there came out a clucking hen with twelve chickens all of gold, and they ran about chirping, and crept again under the old hen's wings. Nothing more beautiful was ever seen in the world! Then she arose, and drove them through the meadow before her, until the bride looked out of the window. The little chickens pleased her so much that she immediately came down and asked if they were for sale. "Not for money or land, but for flesh and blood; let me sleep another night in the chamber where the bridegroom sleeps."

The bride said, "Yes," intending to cheat her as on the former evening.

But when the prince went to bed he asked the page what the murmuring and rustling in the night had been? On this the page told all; that he had been forced to give him a sleeping-draught, because a poor girl had slept secretly in the chamber, and that he was to give him another that night. The prince said, "Pour out the draught by the bed-side."

At night, she was again led in, and when she began to relate how ill all had fared with her, he immediately recognized his beloved wife by her voice, sprang up and cried, "Now I really am released! I have been as it were in a dream, for the strange princess has bewitched me so that I have been compelled to forget thee, but God has delivered me from the spell at the right time." Then they both left the castle secretly in the night, for they feared the father of the princess, who was a sorcerer, and they seated themselves on the griffin which bore them across the Red Sea, and when they were in the midst of it, she let fall the nut. Immediately a tall nut-tree grew up, whereon the bird rested, and then carried them home, where they found their child, who had grown tall and beautiful, and they lived thenceforth happily until their death.

                           ❧

CLEVER HANS

The mother of Hans said, "Whither away, Hans?"
Hans answered, "To Grethel."
"Behave well, Hans."
"Oh, I'll behave well. Good-bye, mother."
"Good-bye, Hans."
Hans comes to Grethel.
"Good day, Grethel."
"Good day, Hans. What dost thou bring that is good?"
"I bring nothing, I want to have something given me."
Grethel presents Hans with a needle.
Hans says, "Good-bye, Grethel."
"Good-bye, Hans."
Hans takes the needle, sticks it into a hay-cart, and follows the cart home.
"Good evening, mother."
"Good evening, Hans. Where hast thou been?"
"With Grethel."
"What didst thou take her?"
"Took nothing; had something given me."
"What did Grethel give thee?"
"Gave me a needle."
"Where is the needle, Hans?"
"Stuck it in the hay-cart."
"That was ill done, Hans. Thou shouldst have stuck the needle in thy sleeve."
"Never mind, I'll do better next time."
"Whither away, Hans?"
"To Grethel, mother."
"Behave well, Hans."
"Oh, I'll behave well. Good-bye, mother."
"Good-bye, Hans."
Hans comes to Grethel. "Good day, Grethel."
"Good day, Hans. What dost thou bring that is good?"

"I bring nothing; I want to have something given to me."

Grethel presents Hans with a knife. "Good-bye, Grethel."

"Good-bye Hans."

Hans takes the knife, sticks it in his sleeve, and goes home.

"Good evening, mother."

"Good evening, Hans. Where hast thou been?"

"With Grethel."

"What didst thou take her?"

"Took her nothing, she gave me something."

"What did Grethel give thee?"

"Gave me a knife."

"Where is the knife, Hans?"

"Stuck in my sleeve."

"That's ill done, Hans, thou shouldst have put the knife in thy pocket."

"Never mind, will do better next time."

"Whither away, Hans?"

"To Grethel, mother."

"Behave well, Hans."

"Oh, I'll behave well. Good-bye, mother."

"Good-bye, Hans."

Hans comes to Grethel. "Good day, Grethel."

"Good day, Hans. What good thing dost thou bring?"

"I bring nothing, I want something given me."

Grethel presents Hans with a young goat. "Good-bye, Grethel."

"Good-bye, Hans."

Hans takes the goat, ties its legs, and puts it in his pocket. When he gets home it is suffocated.

"Good evening, mother."

"Good evening, Hans. Where hast thou been?"

"With Grethel."

"What didst thou take her?"

"Took nothing, she gave me something."

"What did Grethel give thee?"

"She gave me a goat."

"Where is the goat, Hans?"

"Put it in my pocket."

"That was ill done, Hans, thou shouldst have put a rope round the goat's neck."

"Never mind, will do better next time."

"Whither away, Hans?"

"To Grethel, mother."

"Behave well, Hans."

"Oh, I'll behave well. Good-bye, mother."

"Good-bye, Hans."

Hans comes to Grethel.

"Good day, Grethel."

"Good day, Hans. What good thing dost thou bring?"

"I bring nothing, I want something given me."

Grethel presents Hans with a piece of bacon.

"Good-bye, Grethel."

"Good-bye, Hans."

Hans takes the bacon, ties it to a rope, and drags it away behind him. The dogs come and devour the bacon. When he gets home, he has the rope in his hand, and there is no longer anything hanging to it.

"Good evening, mother."

"Good evening, Hans."

"Where hast thou been?"

"With Grethel."

"What didst thou take her?"

"I took her nothing, she gave me something."

"What did Grethel give thee?"

"Gave me a bit of bacon."

"Where is the bacon, Hans?"

"I tied it to a rope, brought it home. Dogs took it."

"That was ill done, Hans, thou shouldst have carried the bacon on thy head."

"Never mind, will do better next time."

"Whither away, Hans?"

"To Grethel, mother."

"Behave well, Hans."

"I'll behave well. Good-bye, mother."

"Good-bye, Hans."

Hans comes to Grethel.
"Good day, Grethel."
"Good day, Hans."
"What good thing dost thou bring?"
"I bring nothing, but would have something given."
Grethel presents Hans with a calf.
"Good-bye, Grethel."
"Good-bye, Hans."
Hans takes the calf, puts it on his head, and the calf kicks his face.
"Good evening, mother."

"Good evening, Hans. Where hast thou been?"

"With Grethel."

"What didst thou take her?"

"I took nothing, but had something given me."

"What did Grethel give thee?"

"A calf."

"Where hast thou the calf, Hans?"

"I set it on my head and it kicked my face."

"That was ill done, Hans, thou shouldst have led the calf, and put it in the stall."

"Never mind, will do better next time."

"Whither away, Hans?"

"To Grethel, mother."

"Behave well, Hans."

"I'll behave well. Good-bye, mother."

"Good-bye, Hans."

Hans comes to Grethel.

"Good day, Grethel."

"Good day, Hans. What good thing dost thou bring?"

"I bring nothing, but would have something given."

Grethel says to Hans, "I will go with thee."

Hans takes Grethel, ties her to a rope, leads her to the rack and binds her fast. Then Hans goes to his mother. "Good evening, mother."

"Good evening, Hans. Where hast thou been?"

"With Grethel."

"What didst thou take her?"

"I took her nothing."

"What did Grethel give thee?"

"She gave me nothing, she came with me."

"Where hast thou left Grethel?"

"I led her by the rope, tied her to the rack, and scattered some grass for her."

"That was ill done, Hans, thou shouldst have cast friendly eyes on her."

When he gets home, he has the rope in his hand,
and there is no longer anything hanging to it

"Never mind, will do better."

Hans went into the stable, cut out all the calves' and sheep's eyes, and threw them in Grethel's face. Then Grethel became angry, tore herself loose and ran away, and never became the bride of Hans.

❧

THE SEVEN RAVENS

There was once a man who had seven sons, and still he had no daughter, however much he wished for one. At length his wife again gave him hope of a child, and when it came into the world it was a girl. The joy was great, but the child was sickly and small, and had to be privately baptized on account of its weakness.

The father sent one of the boys in haste to the spring to fetch water for the baptism. The other six went with him, and as each of them wanted to be first to fill it, the jug fell into the well. There they stood and did not know what to do, and none of them dared to go home.

As they still did not return, the father grew impatient, and said, "They have certainly forgotten it for some game, the wicked boys!"

He became afraid that the girl would have to die without being baptized, and in his anger cried, "I wish the boys were all turned into ravens." Hardly was the word spoken before he heard a whirring of wings over his head in the air, looked up and saw seven coal-black ravens flying away.

The parents could not recall the curse, and however sad they were at the loss of their seven sons, they still to some extent comforted themselves with their dear little daughter, who soon grew strong and every day became more beautiful.

For a long time she did not know that she had had brothers, for her parents were careful not to mention them before her, but one day she accidentally heard some people saying of herself, "that the girl was certainly beautiful, but that in reality she was to blame for the misfortune which had befallen her seven brothers."

Then she was much troubled, and went to her father and mother and asked if it was true that she had had brothers, and what had become of them? The parents now dared keep the secret no longer, but said that what

The good sister took a knife, cut off one of her little fingers, put it in the door, and succeeded in opening it

A little dwarf came to meet her

had befallen her brothers was the will of Heaven, and that her birth had only been the innocent cause. But the maiden took it to heart daily, and thought she must deliver her brothers.

She had no rest or peace until she set out secretly, and went forth into the wide world to trace out her brothers and set them free, let it cost what it might. She took nothing with her but a little ring belonging to her parents as a keepsake, a loaf of bread against hunger, a little pitcher of water against thirst, and a little chair as a provision against weariness.

And now she went continually onwards, far, far to the very end of the world. Then she came to the sun, but it was too hot and terrible, and devoured little children. Hastily she ran away, and ran to the moon, but it was far too cold, and also awful and malicious, and when it saw the child, it said, "I smell, I smell the flesh of men."

On this she ran swiftly away, and came to the stars, which were kind and good to her, and each of them sat on its own particular little chair. But the morning star arose, and gave her the drumstick of a chicken, and said, "If thou hast not that drumstick thou canst not open the Glass Mountain, and in the Glass Mountain are thy brothers."

The maiden took the drumstick, wrapped it carefully in a cloth, and went onwards again until she came to the Glass Mountain. The door was shut, and she thought she would take out the drumstick; but when she undid the cloth, it was empty, and she had lost the good star's present. What was she now to do? She wished to rescue her brothers, and had no key to the Glass Mountain.

The good sister took a knife, cut off one of her little fingers, put it in the door, and succeeded in opening it.

When she had gone inside, a little dwarf came to meet her, who said, "My child, what are you looking for?"

"I am looking for my brothers, the seven ravens," she replied.

The dwarf said, "The lord ravens are not at home, but if you will wait here until they come, step in."

Thereupon the little dwarf carried the ravens' dinner in, on seven little plates, and in seven little glasses, and the little sister ate a morsel from each plate, and from each little glass she took a sip, but in the last little glass she dropped the ring which she had brought away with her.

Suddenly she heard a whirring of wings and a rushing through the air, and then the little dwarf said, "Now the lord ravens are flying home."

Then they came, and wanted to eat and drink, and looked for their little plates and glasses. Then said one after the other, "Who has eaten

Suddenly she heard a whirring of wings and a rushing through the air

"Who has eaten something from my plate? Who has drunk out of my little glass?
It was a human mouth."

something from my plate? Who has drunk out of my little glass? It was a human mouth."

And when the seventh came to the bottom of the glass, the ring rolled against his mouth. Then he looked at it, and saw that it was a ring belonging to his father and mother, and said, "God grant that our sister may be here, and then we shall be free." When the maiden, who was standing behind the door watching, heard that wish, she came forth, and on this all the ravens were restored to their human form again. And they embraced and kissed each other, and went joyfully home.

THE BOY WHO DID NOT FEAR

A certain father had two sons, the elder of whom was smart and sensible, and could do everything. But the younger was stupid and could neither learn nor understand anything, and when people saw him they said, "There's a fellow who will give his father some trouble!"

When anything had to be done, it was always the elder who was forced to do it; but if his father bade him fetch anything when it was late, or in the night-time, and the way led through the churchyard, or any other dismal place, he answered, "Oh, no, father, I'll not go there, it makes me shudder!" for he was afraid. Or when others told stories by the fire at night that made the flesh creep, he sometimes said, "Oh, it makes me shudder!"

The younger sat in a corner and listened with the rest of them, and could not imagine what his older brother meant. "He is always saying 'it makes me shudder, it makes me shudder!' It does not make me shudder," thought he. "That, too, must be an art of which I understand nothing."

Now it came to pass that his father said to younger son one day "Hearken to me, thou fellow in the corner there, thou art growing tall and strong, and thou too must learn something by which thou canst earn thy living. Look how thy brother works, but thou dost not even earn thy salt."

"Well, father," he replied, "I am quite willing to learn something—indeed, if it could but be managed, I should like to learn how to shudder. I don't understand that at all yet."

The elder brother smiled when he heard that, and thought to himself, "Good God, what a blockhead that brother of mine is! He will never be good for anything as long as he lives. He who wants to be a sickle must bend himself betimes."

The father sighed, and answered him, "Thou shalt soon learn what it is to shudder, but thou wilt not earn thy bread by that."

Soon after this the sexton came to the house on a visit, and the father bewailed his trouble, and told him how his younger son was so backward in every respect that he knew nothing and learnt nothing. "Just think," said he, "when I asked him how he was going to earn his bread, he actually wanted to learn to shudder."

"If that be all," replied the sexton, "he can learn that with me. Send him to me, and I will soon polish him."

The father was glad to do it, for he thought, "It will train the boy a little."

The sexton therefore took him into his house, and he had to ring the bell. After a day or two, the sexton awoke him at midnight, and bade him arise and go up into the church tower and ring the bell. "Thou shalt soon learn what shuddering is," thought he, and secretly went there before him; and when the boy was at the top of the tower and turned round, and was just going to take hold of the bell rope, he saw a white figure standing on the stairs opposite the sounding hole. "Who is there?" cried he, but the figure made no reply, and did not move or stir. "Give an answer," cried the boy, "or take thy self off, thou hast no business here at night."

The sexton, however, remained standing motionless that the boy might think he was a ghost. The boy cried a second time, "What do you want here?—speak if thou art an honest fellow, or I will throw thee down the steps!"

The sexton thought, "he can't intend to be as bad as his words," uttered no sound and stood as if he were made of stone. Then the boy called to him for the third time, and as that was also to no purpose, the boy ran against the ghost and pushed it down the stairs, so that it fell down ten steps and remained lying there in a corner.

Thereupon he rang the bell, went home, and without saying a word went to bed, and fell asleep.

The sexton's wife waited a long time for her husband, but he did not come back. At length she became uneasy, and wakened the boy, and asked,

"Dost thou not know where my husband is? He climbed up the tower before thou didst."

"No, I don't know," replied the boy, "but someone was standing by the sounding hole on the other side of the steps, and as he would neither give an answer nor go away, I took him for a scoundrel, and threw him downstairs. Just go there and you will see if it was he. I should be sorry if it were." The woman ran away and found her husband, who was lying moaning in the corner, and had broken his leg.

She carried him down, and then with loud screams she hastened to the boy's father. "Your boy," cried she, "has been the cause of a great misfortune! He has thrown my husband down the steps and made him break his leg. Take the good-for-nothing fellow away from our house."

The father was terrified and ran thither and scolded the boy. "What wicked tricks are these?" said he, "the devil must have put this into thy head."

"Father," he replied, "do listen to me. I am quite innocent. He was standing there by night like one who is intending to do some evil. I did not know who it was, and I entreated him three times either to speak or to go away."

"Ah," said the father, "I have nothing but unhappiness with you. Go out of my sight. I will see thee no more."

"Yes, father, right willingly, wait only until it is day. Then will I go forth and learn how to shudder, and then I shall, at any rate, understand one art which will support me." "Learn what thou wilt," spake the father, "it is all the same to me. Here are fifty thalers for thee. Take these and go into the wide world, and tell no one from whence thou comest, and who is thy father, for I have reason to be ashamed of thee." "Yes, father, it shall be as you will. If you desire nothing more than that, I can easily keep it in mind."

When day dawned, therefore, the boy put his fifty thalers into his pocket, and went forth on the great highway, and continually said to himself, "If I could but shudder! If I could but shudder!"

Then a man approached who heard this conversation which the youth was holding with himself, and when they had walked a little farther to where they could see the gallows, the man said to him, "Look, there is the tree where seven men have married the ropemaker's daughter, and are now learning how to fly. Sit down below it, and wait till night comes, and you will soon learn how to shudder."

"If that is all that is wanted," answered the youth, "it is easily done; but if I learn how to shudder as fast as that, thou shalt have my fifty thalers. Just come back to me early in the morning."

Then the youth went to the gallows, sat down below it, and waited till evening came. And as he was cold, he lighted himself a fire, but at midnight the wind blew so sharply that in spite of his fire, he could not get warm.

And as the wind knocked the hanged men against each other, and they moved backwards and forwards, he thought to himself, "Thou shiverest below by the fire, but how those up above must freeze and suffer!" And as he felt pity for them, he raised the ladder, and climbed up, unbound one of them after the other, and brought down all seven. Then he stirred the fire, blew it, and set them all round it to warm themselves. But they sat there and did not stir, and the fire caught their clothes.

So he said, "Take care, or I will hang you up again." The dead men, however, did not hear, but were quite silent, and let their rags go on burning. On this he grew angry, and said, "If you will not take care, I cannot help you, I will not be burnt with you," and he hung them up again each in his turn.

Then he sat down by his fire and fell asleep, and the next morning the man came to him and wanted to have the fifty thalers, and said, "Well, dost thou know how to shudder?"

"No," answered he, "how was I to get to know? Those fellows up there did not open their mouths, and were so stupid that they let the few old rags which they had on their bodies get burnt." Then the man saw that he would not get the fifty thalers that day, and went away saying, "One of this kind has never come my way before."

The youth likewise went his way, and once more began to mutter to himself, "Ah, if I could but shudder! Ah, if I could but shudder!"

A wagoner who was striding behind him heard that and asked, "Who are you?"

"I don't know," answered the youth.

Then the wagoner asked, "From whence comest thou?"

"I know not."

"Who is thy father?"

"That I may not tell thee."

"What is it that thou art always muttering between thy teeth."

"Ah," replied the youth, "I do so wish I could shudder, but no one can teach me how to do it."

"Give up thy foolish chatter," said the wagoner. "Come, go with me, I will see about a place for thee."

The youth went with the wagoner, and in the evening they arrived at an inn where they wished to pass the night. Then at the entrance of the room the youth again said quite loudly, "If I could but shudder! If I could but shudder!"

The host who heard this, laughed and said, "If that is your desire, there ought to be a good opportunity for you here."

"Ah, be silent," said the hostess, "so many inquisitive persons have already lost their lives, it would be a pity and a shame if such beautiful eyes as these should never see the daylight again."

But the youth said, "However difficult it may be, I will learn it and for this purpose indeed have I journeyed forth."

He let the host have no rest, until the latter told him, that not far from thence stood a haunted castle where any one could very easily learn what shuddering was, if he would but watch in it for three nights. The King had promised that he who would venture should have his daughter to wife, and she was the most beautiful maiden the sun shone on. Great treasures likewise lay in the castle, which were guarded by evil spirits, and these treasures would then be freed, and would make a poor man rich enough. Already many men had gone into the castle, but as yet none had come out again.

Then the youth went next morning to the King and said if he were allowed he would watch three nights in the haunted castle. The King looked at him, and as the youth pleased him, he said, "Thou mayest ask for three things to take into the castle with thee, but they must be things without life."

Then he answered, "Then I ask for a fire, a turning lathe, and a cutting-board with the knife."

The King had these things carried into the castle for him during the day. When night was drawing near, the youth went up and made himself a bright fire in one of the rooms, placed the cutting-board and knife beside it, and seated himself by the turning-lathe. "Ah, if I could but shudder!" said he, "but I shall not learn it here either."

Towards midnight he was about to poke his fire, and as he was blowing it, something cried suddenly from one corner, "Au, miau! how cold we are!"

"You simpletons!" cried he, "what are you crying about? If you are cold, come and take a seat by the fire and warm yourselves."

And when he had said that, two great black cats came with one tremendous leap and sat down on each side of him, and looked savagely at him with their fiery eyes. After a short time, when they had warmed themselves, they said, "Comrade, shall we have a game at cards?"

"Why not?" he replied, "but just show me your paws."

Then they stretched out their claws. "Oh," said he, "what long nails you have! Wait, I must first cut them for you." Thereupon he seized them by the throats, put them on the cutting-board and screwed their feet fast. "I have looked at your fingers," said he, "and my fancy for card-playing has gone," and he struck them dead and threw them out into the water.

But when he had made away with these two, and was about to sit down again by his fire, out from every hole and corner came black cats and black dogs with red-hot chains, and more and more of them came until he could no longer stir, and they yelled horribly, and got on his fire, pulled it to pieces,

Out from every hole and corner came black cats and black dogs

and tried to put it out. He watched them for a while quietly, but at last when they were going too far, he seized his cutting-knife, and cried, "Away with ye, vermin," and began to cut them down. Part of them ran away, the others he killed, and threw out into the fish-pond.

When he came back he fanned the embers of his fire again and warmed himself. And as he thus sat, his eyes would keep open no longer, and he felt a desire to sleep. Then he looked round and saw a great bed in the corner. "That is the very thing for me," said he, and got into it. When he was just going to shut his eyes, however, the bed began to move of its own accord, and went over the whole of the castle.

"That's right," said he, "but go faster." Then the bed rolled on as if six horses were harnessed to it, up and down, over thresholds and steps, but suddenly hop, hop, it turned over upside down, and lay on him like a mountain. But he threw quilts and pillows up in the air, got out and said, "Now any one who likes, may drive," and lay down by his fire, and slept till it was day.

In the morning the King came, and when he saw him lying there on the ground, he thought the evil spirits had killed him and he was dead. Then said he, "After all it is a pity—he is a handsome man."

The youth heard it, got up, and said, "It has not come to that yet." Then the King was astonished, but very glad, and asked how he had fared. "Very well indeed," answered he; "one night is past, the two others will get over likewise."

Then he went to the innkeeper, who opened his eyes very wide, and said, "I never expected to see thee alive again! Hast thou learnt how to shudder yet?" "No," said he, "it is all in vain. If some one would but tell me."

The second night he again went up into the old castle, sat down by the fire, and once more began his old song, "If I could but shudder."

When midnight came, an uproar and noise of tumbling about was heard; at first it was low, but it grew louder and louder. Then it was quiet for awhile, and at length with a loud scream, half a man came down the chimney and fell before him.

"Hollo!" cried he, "another half belongs to this. This is too little!" Then the uproar began again, there was a roaring and howling, and the other half fell down likewise.

"Wait," said he, "I will just blow up the fire a little for thee." When he had done that and looked round again, the two pieces were joined together, and a frightful man was sitting in his place. "That is no part of our bargain," said the youth, "the bench is mine."

The man wanted to push him away; the youth, however, would not allow that, but thrust him off with all his strength, and seated himself again in his own place.

Then still more men fell down, one after the other; they brought nine dead men's legs and two skulls, and set them up and played at nine-pins with them.

The youth also wanted to play and said "Hark you, can I join you?"

"Yes, if thou hast any money."

"Money enough," replied he, "but your balls are not quite round." Then he took the skulls and put them in the lathe and turned them till they were round. "There, now, they will roll better!" said he. "Hurrah! Now it goes merrily!"

He played with them and lost some of his money, but when it struck twelve, everything vanished from his sight. He lay down and quietly fell asleep. Next morning the King came to inquire after him. "How has it fared with you this time?" asked he.

"I have been playing at nine-pins," he answered, "and have lost a couple of farthings."

"Hast thou not shuddered then?"

"Eh, what?" said he, "I have made merry. If I did but know what it was to shudder!"

The third night he sat down again on his bench and said quite sadly, "If I could but shudder."

When it grew late, six tall men came in and brought a coffin. Then said he, "Ha, ha, that is certainly my little cousin, who died only a few days ago," and he beckoned with his finger, and cried "Come, little cousin, come."

They placed the coffin on the ground, but he went to it and took the lid off, and a dead man lay therein. He felt his face, but it was cold as ice. "Stop," said he, "I will warm thee a little," and went to the fire and warmed his hand and laid it on the dead man's face, but he remained cold.

Then he took him out, and sat down by the fire and laid him on his breast and rubbed his arms that the blood might circulate again. As this also did no good, he thought to himself "When two people lie in bed together, they warm each other," and carried him to the bed, covered him over and lay

*Then the youth seized the ax, split the anvil with one blow,
and struck the old man's beard in with it*

down by him. After a short time the dead man became warm, too, and began to move. Then said the youth, "See, little cousin, have I not warmed thee?"

The dead man, however, got up and cried, "Now will I strangle thee."

"What!" said he, "is that the way thou thankest me? Thou shalt at once go into thy coffin again," and he took him up, threw him into it, and shut the lid. Then came the six men and carried him away again.

"I cannot manage to shudder," said he. "I shall never learn it here as long as I live."

Then a man entered who was taller than all others, and looked terrible. He was old, however, and had a long white beard. "Thou wretch," cried he, "thou shalt soon learn what it is to shudder, for thou shalt die."

"Not so fast," replied the youth. "If I am to die, I shall have to have a say in it."

"I will soon seize thee," said the fiend.

"Softly, softly, do not talk so big. I am as strong as thou art, and perhaps even stronger."

"We shall see," said the old man. "If thou art stronger, I will let thee go— come, we will try."

Then he led him by dark passages to a smith's forge, took an ax, and with one blow struck an anvil into the ground.

"I can do better than that," said the youth, and went to the other anvil. The old man placed himself near and wanted to look on, and his white beard hung down.

Then the youth seized the ax, split the anvil with one blow, and struck the old man's beard in with it. "Now I have thee," said the youth.

"Now it is thou who will have to die." Then he seized an iron bar and beat the old man till he moaned, and entreated him to stop, and said he would give him great riches.

The youth drew out the ax and let him go. The old man led him back into the castle, and in a cellar showed him three chests full of gold. "Of these," said he, "one part is for the poor, the other for the King, the third is thine."

In the meantime it struck twelve, and the spirit disappeared. The youth, therefore, was left in darkness.

"I shall still be able to find my way out," said he, and felt about, found the way into the room, and slept there by his fire.

Next morning the King came and said "Now thou must have learnt what shuddering is?"

"No," he answered; "what can it be? My dead cousin was here, and a bearded man came and showed me a great deal of money down below, but no one told me what it was to shudder."

"Then," said the King, "thou hast delivered the castle, and shalt marry my daughter."

"That is all very well," said he, "but still I do not know what it is to shudder."

Then the gold was brought up and the wedding celebrated; but howsoever much the young king loved his wife, and however happy he was, he still said always "If I could but shudder—if I could but shudder."

And at last she was angry at this. Her waiting-maid said, "I will find a cure for him; he shall soon learn what it is to shudder." She went out to the stream which flowed through the garden, and had a whole bucketful of gudgeons brought to her.

At night when the young king was sleeping, his wife was to draw the clothes off him and empty the bucketful of cold water with the gudgeons in it over him, so that the little fishes would sprawl about him.

When this was done, he woke up and cried "Oh, what makes me shudder so, what makes me shudder so, dear wife? Ah! now I know what it is to shudder!"

❧

CLEVER ELSIE

There was once a man who had a daughter who was called Clever Elsie. And when she had grown up her father said, "We will get her married."

"Yes," said the mother; "if only any one would come who would have her."

At length a man came from a distance and wooed her, who was called Hans; but he stipulated that Clever Elsie should be really wise.

"Oh," said the father, "she's sharp enough."

And the mother said, "Oh, she can see the wind coming up the street, and hear the flies coughing."

"Well," said Hans, "if she is not really wise, I won't have her."

When they were sitting at dinner and had eaten, the mother said, "Elsie, go into the cellar and fetch some beer."

Then Clever Elsie took the pitcher from the wall, went into the cellar, and tapped the lid briskly as she went, so that the time might not appear long. When she was below she fetched herself a chair, and set it before the barrel so that she had no need to stoop, and did not hurt her back or do herself any unexpected injury. Then she placed the can before her, and turned the tap, and while the beer was running she would not let her eyes be idle, but looked up at the wall, and after much peering here and there, saw a pickax exactly above her, which the masons had accidentally left there.

Then Clever Elsie began to weep, and said, "If I get Hans, and we have a child, and he grows big, and we send him into the cellar here to draw beer, then the pickax will fall on his head and kill him."

Then she sat and wept and screamed with all the strength of her body, over the misfortune which lay before her. Those upstairs waited for the drink, but Clever Elsie still did not come. Then the woman said to the servant, "Just go down into the cellar and see where Elsie is."

The maid went and found her sitting in front of the barrel, screaming loudly. "Elsie, why weepest thou?" asked the maid.

"Ah," she answered, "have I not reason to weep? If I get Hans, and we have a child, and he grows big, and has to draw beer here, the pickax will perhaps fall on his head, and kill him."

She would not let her eyes be idle, but looked up at the wall, and after much peering here and there, saw a pickax exactly above her, which the masons had accidentally left there

Then said the maid, "What a clever Elsie we have!" and sat down beside her and began loudly to weep over the misfortune.

After a while, as the maid did not come back, those upstairs were thirsty for the beer, the man said to the boy, "Just go down into the cellar and see where Elsie and the girl are."

The boy went down, and there sat Clever Elsie and the girl both weeping together. Then he asked, "Why are ye weeping?"

"Ah," said Elsie, "have I not reason to weep? If I get Hans, and we have a child, and he grows big, and has to draw beer here, the pickax will fall on his head and kill him." Then said the boy, "What a clever Elsie we have!" and sat down by her, and likewise began to howl loudly.

Upstairs they waited for the boy, but as he still did not return, the man said to the woman, "Just go down into the cellar and see where Elsie is!"

The woman went down, and found all three in the midst of their lamentations, and inquired what was the cause; then Elsie told her also that her future child was to be killed by the pickax, when it grew big and had to draw beer, and the pickax fell down. Then said the mother likewise, "What a clever Elsie we have!" and sat down and wept with them.

The man upstairs waited a short time, but as his wife did not come back and his thirst grew ever greater, he said, "I must go into the cellar myself and see where Elsie is."

But when he got into the cellar, and they were all sitting together crying, and he heard the reason, and that Elsie's child was the cause, and that Elsie might perhaps bring one into the world some day, and that it might be killed by the pickax, if it should happen to be sitting beneath it, drawing beer just at the very time when it fell down, he cried, "Oh, what a clever Elsie!" and sat down, and likewise wept with them.

The bridegroom stayed upstairs alone for a long time; then as no one would come back he thought, "They must be waiting for me below; I too must go there and see what they are about." When he got down, five of them were sitting screaming and lamenting quite piteously, each out-doing the other. "What misfortune has happened then?" he asked.

"Ah, dear Hans," said Elsie, "if we marry each other and have a child, and he is big, and we perhaps send him here to draw something to drink, then the pickax which has been left up there might dash his brains out if it were to fall down, so have we not reason to weep?"

"Come," said Hans, "more understanding than that is not needed for my household, as thou art such a clever Elsie, I will have thee," and he seized her hand, took her upstairs with him, and married her.

After Hans had had her some time, he said, "Wife, I am going out to work and earn some money for us; go into the field and cut the corn that we may have some bread."

"Yes, dear Hans, I will do that."

After Hans had gone away, she cooked herself some good broth and took it into the field with her. When she came to the field she said to herself, "What shall I do; shall I shear first, or shall I eat first? Oh, I will eat first." Then she emptied her basin of broth, and when she was fully satisfied, she once more said, "What shall I do? Shall I shear first, or shall I sleep first? I will sleep first." Then she lay down among the corn and fell asleep.

Hans had been at home for a long time, but Elsie did not come; then said he, "What a clever Elsie I have; she is so industrious that she does not even come home to eat."

As, however, she still stayed away, and it was evening, Hans went out to see what she had cut, but nothing was cut, and she was lying among the corn asleep. Then Hans hastened home and brought a fowler's net with little bells and hung it round about her, and she still went on sleeping. Then he ran home, shut the house-door, and sat down in his chair and worked.

At length, when it was quite dark, Clever Elsie awoke and when she got up there was a jingling all round about her, and the bells rang at each step which she took. Then she was alarmed, and became uncertain whether she really was Clever Elsie or not, and said, "Is it I, or is it not I?" But she knew not what answer to make to this, and stood for a time in doubt; at length she thought, "I will go home and ask if it be I, or if it be not I, they will be sure to know."

She ran to the door of her own house, but it was shut; then she knocked at the window and cried, "Hans, is Elsie within?"

"Yes," answered Hans, "she is within."

Hereupon she was terrified, and said, "Ah, heavens! Then it is not I," and went to another door; but when the people heard the jingling of the bells they would not open it, and she could get in nowhere. Then she ran out of the village, and no one has seen her since.

THE FOUR SKILLFUL BROTHERS

There was once a poor man who had four sons, and when they were grown up, he said to them, "My dear children, you must now go out into the world, for I have nothing to give you, so set out, and go some distance to learn a trade, and see how you can make your way."

So the four brothers took their sticks, bade their father farewell, and went through the town-gate together. When they had traveled about for some time, they came to a cross-way which branched off in four different directions. Then said the eldest, "Here we must separate, but on this day four years hence, we will meet each other again at this spot, and in the meantime we will seek our fortunes." Then each of them went his way.

The eldest met a man who asked him where he was going, and what he was intending to do? "I want to learn a trade," he replied. Then the other said, "Come with me and be a thief." "No," he answered, "that is not regarded as a reputable trade, and the end of it is that one has to swing on the gallows." "Oh," said the man, "you need not be afraid of the gallows; I will only teach you to get such things as no other man could ever lay hold of, and no one will ever detect you." So he allowed himself to be talked into it, and he became an accomplished thief, and so dexterous that nothing was safe from him once he desired to have it.

The second brother met a man who put the same question to him about what he wanted to learn in the world. "I don't know yet," he replied. "Then come with me, and be an astronomer; there is nothing better than that, for nothing is hid from you." He liked the idea, and became such a skillful astronomer that when he had learned everything and was about to travel onwards, his master gave him a telescope and said to him, "With that canst thou see whatsoever takes place either on earth or in heaven, and nothing can remain concealed from thee."

A huntsman took the third brother into training and gave him such excellent instruction in everything which related to huntsmanship that he became an experienced hunter. When he went away, his master gave him a gun and said, "It will never fail you; whatsoever you aim at, you are certain to hit it."

So the four brothers took their sticks, bade their father farewell,
and went through the town-gate together

The youngest brother also met a man who spoke to him, and inquired what his intentions were. "Would you not like to be a tailor?" said he. "Not that I know of," said the youth; "sitting doubled up from morning till night, driving the needle and the goose backwards and forwards, is not to my taste." "Oh, but you are speaking in ignorance," answered the man. "With me you would learn a very different kind of tailoring, which is respectable and proper, and for the most part very honorable." So he let himself be persuaded, and went with the man, and learned his art from the very beginning. When they parted, the man gave the youth a needle and said, "With this you can sew together whatever is given you, whether it is as soft as an egg or as hard as steel; and it will all become one piece of stuff, so that no seam will be visible."

When the appointed four years were over, the four brothers arrived at the same time at the cross-roads, embraced and kissed each other, and returned home to their father. "So now," said he, quite delighted, "the wind has blown you back again to me." While they sat in front of the house under a large tree, they told him of all that had happened to them, and how each had learned his own trade. "Now," the father said, "I will put you all to the test and see what you can do."

Then he looked up and said to his second son, "Between two branches up at the top of this tree, there is a chaffinch's nest. Tell me how many eggs there are in it?" The astronomer took his glass, looked up, and said, "There are five." Then the father said to the eldest, "Fetch the eggs down without disturbing the bird which is sitting hatching them." The skillful thief climbed up, took the five eggs from beneath the bird—which never observed what he was doing and remained quietly sitting where she was—and brought them down to his father. The father took them, and put one of them on each corner of the table, and the fifth in the middle, and said to the huntsman, "With one shot thou shalt shoot all five eggs in two, through the middle." The huntsman aimed, and shot the eggs, all five as the father had desired, and that at one shot. "Now it's your turn," said the father to the fourth son. "You shall sew the eggs together again, and the young birds that are inside them as well, so that they are not hurt by the shot." The tailor brought his needle, and sewed them as his father wished. When he had done this the thief had to climb up the tree again, and carry them to the nest, and put them back again under the bird without her being aware of it. The bird sat her full time, and after a few days the young ones crept out, and they had a red line round their necks where they had been sewn together by the tailor.

"Well," said the old man to his sons, "I begin to think you are worth more than breen clover. You have used your time well and learned something good. I can't say which of you deserves the most praise. That will be proved if you have but an early opportunity of using your talents."

Not long after this, there was a great uproar in the country when the King's daughter was carried off by a dragon. The King was full of trouble about it, both by day and night, and he proclaimed that whosoever brought her back should have her as his wife. The four brothers said to themselves, "This would be a fine opportunity for us to show what we can do!" and they resolved to go forth together and liberate the King's daughter. "I will soon know where she is," said the astronomer, and he looked through his telescope and said, "I see her already; she is far away from here on a rock in the sea, and the dragon is beside her, watching her."

Then he went to the King, and asked for a ship for himself and his brothers, and sailed with them over the sea until they came to the rock. There the King's daughter was sitting, and the dragon was lying asleep on her lap. The huntsman said, "I dare not fire, I should kill the beautiful maiden at the same time." "Then I will try my art," said the thief, and he crept thither and stole her away from under the dragon, so quietly and dexterously, that the monster never remarked it, but went on snoring. Full of joy, they hurried off with her on board ship, and steered out into the open sea. But when the dragon awoke and found the princess gone, he followed them, and came snorting angrily through the air. Just as he was circling above the ship, and about to descend on it, the huntsman shouldered his gun, and shot the monster to the heart. It fell down dead, but was so large and powerful that his fall shattered the whole ship. Although they laid hold of several planks to float upon the wide sea, they were in great peril. But the tailor was not idle: he took his wondrous needle and, with a few stitches, sewed the planks together. After they had seated themselves upon them and collected together all the fragments of the vessel, he sewed these so skillfully together that, in a very short time, the ship was once more seaworthy, and they could go home again in safety.

When the King once more saw his daughter, there were great rejoicings. He said to the four brothers, "One of you shall have her to wife, but which

The King's daughter was carried off by a dragon

There the King's daughter was sitting, and the dragon was lying asleep on her lap

of you it is to be you must settle among yourselves." Then a contest began among them, for each preferred his own claim. The astronomer said, "If I had not seen the princess, all your arts would have been useless, so she is mine." The thief said, "What would have been the use of your seeing, if I had not gotten her away from the dragon? so she is mine." The huntsman said, "The princess and all of you would have been torn to pieces by the dragon if my shot had not hit him, so she is mine." The tailor said, "And if I, by my art, had not sewn the ship together again, you would all of you have been miserably drowned, so she is mine." Then the King uttered this saying, "Each of you has an equal right, and as all of you cannot have the maiden, none of you shall have her, but I will give to each of you, as a reward, a portion of my kingdom." The brothers were pleased with this decision, and said, "It is better thus than that we should be at variance with each other." Then each of them received his portion, and they lived with their father in the greatest happiness as long as it pleased God.

CLEVER GRETHEL

There was once a cook named Grethel who wore shoes with red rosettes, and when she walked out with them on she turned herself this way and that, and thought, "You certainly are a pretty girl!" And when she came home she drank, in her gladness of heart, a draught of wine. And as wine excites a desire to eat, she tasted the best of whatever she was cooking until she was satisfied, and said, "The cook must know what the food is like."

It came to pass that the master one day said to her, "Grethel, there is a guest coming this evening; prepare me two fowls very daintily."

"I will see to it, master," answered Grethel.

She killed two fowls, scalded them, plucked them, put them on the spit, and towards evening set them before the fire, that they might roast. The fowls began to turn brown, and were nearly ready, but the guest had not yet arrived.

Then Grethel called out to her master, "If the guest does not come, I must take the fowls away from the fire, but it will be a sin and a shame if they are not eaten directly, when they are juiciest."

The master said, "I will run myself, and fetch the guest."

When the master had turned his back, Grethel laid the spit with the fowls on one side, and thought, "Standing so long by the fire there makes one hot and thirsty; who knows when they will come? Meanwhile, I will run into the cellar and take a drink." She ran down, set a jug, said, "God bless it to thy use, Grethel," took a good drink, and took yet another hearty draught

Then she went and put the fowls down again to the fire, basted them, and drove the spit merrily round. But as the roast meat smelt so good, Grethel thought, "Something might be wrong, it ought to be tasted!" She touched it with her finger, and said, "Ah! how good fowls are! It certainly is a sin and a shame that they are not eaten directly!"

She ran to the window, to see if the master was coming with his guest, but she saw no one, and went back to the fowls and thought, "One of the wings is burning! I had better take it off and eat it." So she cut it off, ate it, and enjoyed it, and when she had done, she thought, "the other must go down too, or else master will observe that something is missing."

When the two wings were eaten, she went and looked for her master, and did not see him. Then she thought, "Who knows? Perhaps they are not coming at all, and have turned in somewhere." Then she said, "Hallo, Grethel, enjoy yourself, one fowl has been cut into, take another drink, and eat it up entirely. When it is eaten you will have some peace. Why should God's good gifts be spoiled?" So she ran into the cellar again, took an enormous drink and ate up the one chicken in great glee. When one of the chickens was swallowed down, and still her master did not come, Grethel looked at the other and said, "Where one is, the other should be likewise, the two go together; what's right for the one is right for the other. I think if I were to take another draught it would do me no harm." So she took another hearty drink, and let the second chicken join the first.

While she was just in the best of the eating, her master came and cried, "Haste thee, Grethel, the guest is coming directly after me!"

"Yes, sir, I will soon serve up," answered Grethel. Meantime the master looked to see that the table was properly laid, and took the great knife, wherewith he was going to carve the chickens, and sharpened it on the steps. Presently the guest came, and knocked politely and courteously at the house-door. Grethel ran, and looked to see who was there, and when she saw the guest, she put her finger to her lips and said, "Hush! hush! get away as quickly as you can. If my master catches you it will be the worse for you.

He ran after him with the knife still in his hand, crying, "Just one, just one."

He certainly did ask you to supper, but his intention is to cut off your two ears. Just listen how he is sharpening the knife for it!"

The guest heard the sharpening, and hurried down the steps again as fast as he could. Grethel was not idle; she ran screaming to her master, and cried, "You have invited a fine guest!"

"Eh, why, Grethel? What do you mean by that?"

"Yes," said she, "he has taken the chickens which I was just going to serve up, off the dish, and has run away with them!"

"That's a nice trick!" said her master, and lamented the fine chickens. "If he had but left me one, so that something remained for me to eat." He called to him to stop, but the guest pretended not to hear. Then he ran after him with the knife still in his hand, crying, "Just one, just one," meaning that the guest should leave him just one chicken, and not take both. The guest, however, thought no otherwise than that he was to give up one of his ears, and ran as if fire were burning under him, in order to take them both home with him.

THE BREMEN TOWN-MUSICIANS

A certain man had a donkey, which had carried the corn-sacks to the mill indefatigably for many a long year; but his strength was going, and he was growing more and more unfit for work. Then his master began to consider how he might best save his keep; but the donkey, seeing that no good wind was blowing, ran away and set out on the road to Bremen. "There," he thought, "I can surely be town-musician."

When he had walked some distance, he found a hound lying on the road, gasping like one who had run till he was tired. "What are you gasping so for, you big fellow?" asked the donkey.

"Ah," replied the hound, "as I am old, and daily grow weaker, and no longer can hunt, my master wanted to kill me, so I took to flight; but now how am I to earn my bread?"

"I'll tell you what," said the donkey, "I am going to Bremen, and shall be town-musician there; go with me and engage yourself also as a musician. I will play the lute, and you shall beat the kettledrum." The hound agreed, and on they went.

Before long they came to a cat, sitting on the path, with a face like three rainy days. "Now then, old shaver, what has gone askew with you?" asked the donkey.

"Who can be merry when his neck is in danger?" answered the cat. "Because I am now getting old, and my teeth are worn to stumps, and I prefer to sit by the fire and spin, rather than hunt about after mice, my mistress wanted to drown me, so I ran away. But now good advice is scarce. Where am I to go?"

"Go with us to Bremen. You understand night-music, you can be a town-musician." The cat thought well of it, and went with them.

Before long they came to a cat, sitting on the path, with a face like three rainy days

After this the three fugitives came to a farm-yard, where the cock was sitting upon the gate, crowing with all his might. "Your crow goes through and through one," said the donkey. "What is the matter?"

"I have been foretelling fine weather, because it is the day on which Our Lady washes the Christ-child's little shirts, and wants to dry them," said the cock; "but guests are coming for Sunday, so the housewife has no pity, and has told the cook that she intends to put me in the soup tomorrow. This evening I am to have my head cut off. Now I am crowing at full pitch while I can."

"Ah, but red-comb," said the donkey, "you had better come away with us. We are going to Bremen; you can find something better than death everywhere: you have a good voice, and if we make music together it must have some quality!"

The cock agreed to this plan, and all four went on together. They could not, however, reach the city of Bremen in one day, and in the evening they came to a forest where they meant to pass the night. The donkey and the hound laid themselves down under a large tree, the cat and the cock settled themselves in the branches; but the cock flew right to the top, where he was most safe. Before he went to sleep he looked round on all four sides, and thought he saw in the distance a little spark burning; so he called out to his companions that there must be a house not far off, for he saw a light. The donkey said, "If so, we had better get up and go on, for the shelter here is bad." The hound thought that a few bones with some meat on would do him good too.

So they made their way to the place where the light was, and found it to be to a well-lighted robbers' house. The donkey, as the biggest, went to the window and looked in.

"What do you see, my gray-horse?" asked the cock. "What do I see?" answered the donkey. "A table covered with good things to eat and drink, and robbers sitting at it enjoying themselves." "That would be the sort of thing for us," said the cock. "Yes, yes; ah, how I wish we were there!" said the donkey.

Then the animals took counsel together how they should manage to drive away the robbers, and at last they thought of a plan. The donkey was to place himself with his fore-feet upon the window-ledge, the hound was to jump on the donkey's back, the cat was to climb upon the dog, and lastly the cock was to fly up and perch upon the head of the cat. When this was done, at a given signal, they began to perform their music together: the donkey brayed, the hound barked, the cat mewed, and the cock crowed; then they burst through the window into the room, so that the glass clattered! At this horrible din, the robbers sprang up, thinking no otherwise than that a ghost had come in, and fled in a great fright out into the forest. The four companions now sat down at the table, well content with what was left, and ate as if they were going to fast for a month.

As soon as the four minstrels had done, they put out the light, and each sought for himself a sleeping-place according to his nature and to what suited him. The donkey laid himself down upon some straw in the yard, the hound behind the door, the cat upon the hearth near the warm ashes, and the cock perched himself upon a beam of the roof; and being tired from their long walk, they soon went to sleep.

When it was past midnight, and the robbers saw from afar that the light was no longer burning in their house, and all appeared quiet, the captain said, "We ought not to have let ourselves be frightened out of our wits"; and he ordered one of them to go and examine the house.

The messenger, finding all still, went into the kitchen to light a candle, and, taking the glistening fiery eyes of the cat for live coals, he held a lucifer-match to them to light it. But the cat did not understand the joke, and flew in his face, spitting and scratching. He was dreadfully frightened, and ran to the back-door, but the dog, who lay there sprang up and bit his leg; and as he ran across the yard by the straw-heap, the donkey gave him a smart kick with its hind foot. The cock, too, who had been awakened by the noise, and had become lively, cried down from the beam, "Cock-a-doodle-doo!"

The donkey brayed, the hound barked, the cat mewed, and the cock crowed

Then the robber ran back as fast as he could to his captain, and said, "Ah, there is a horrible witch sitting in the house who spat on me and scratched my face with her long claws; and by the door stands a man with a knife, who stabbed me in the leg; and in the yard there lies a black monster, who beat me with a wooden club; and above, upon the roof, sits the judge, who called out, 'Bring the rogue here to me!' So I got away as well as I could."

After this the robbers did not trust themselves in the house again; but it suited the four musicians of Bremen so well that they did not care to leave it any more.

THE WATER OF LIFE

There was once a king who had an illness, and no one believed that he would come out of it with his life. He had three sons who were much distressed about it, and went down into the palace-garden and wept. There they met an old man who inquired as to the cause of their grief. They told him that their father was so ill that he would most certainly die, for nothing seemed to cure him. Then the old man said, "I know of one more remedy, and that is the water of life. If he drinks of it he will become well again; but it is hard to find."

The eldest said, "I will manage to find it," and went to the sick King, and begged to be allowed to go forth in search of the water of life, for that alone could save him.

"No," said the King, "the danger of it is too great. I would rather die." But he begged so long that the King consented.

The prince thought in his heart, "If I bring the water, then I shall be best beloved of my father, and shall inherit the kingdom."

So he set out, and when he had ridden forth a little distance, a dwarf stood there in the road who called to him and said, "Whither away so fast?"

"Silly shrimp," said the prince, very haughtily, "it is nothing to do with you," and rode on. But the little dwarf grew angry, and he wished an evil wish. Soon after this the prince entered a ravine, and the further he rode the closer the mountains drew together. And at last the road became so narrow that he could not advance a step further; it was impossible either to turn his horse or to dismount from the saddle, and he was shut in there as if in prison. The sick King waited long for him, but he came not.

Then the second son said, "Father, let me go forth to seek the water," and thought to himself, "If my brother is dead, then the kingdom will fall to me." At first the King would not allow him to go either, but at last he yielded, so the prince set out on the same road that his brother had taken, and he too met the dwarf, who stopped him to ask, whither he was going in such haste?

"Little shrimp," said the prince, "that is nothing to thee," and rode on without giving him another look. But the dwarf bewitched him, and he, like the other, rode into a ravine, and could neither go forwards nor backwards. So fare haughty people.

As the second son also remained away, the youngest begged to be allowed to go forth to fetch the water, and at last the King was obliged to let him go. When he met the dwarf and the latter asked him whither he was going in such haste, he stopped, gave him an explanation, and said, "I am seeking the water of life, for my father is sick unto death."

"Dost thou know, then, where it is to be found?"

"No," said the prince.

"As thou hast borne thyself as is seemly, and not haughtily like thy false brothers, I will give thee the information and tell thee how thou mayst obtain the water of life. It springs from a fountain in the courtyard of an enchanted castle, but thou wilt not be able to make thy way to it, if I do not give thee an iron wand and two small loaves of bread. Strike thrice with the wand on the iron door of the castle and it will spring open: inside lie two lions with gaping jaws, but if thou throwest a loaf to each of them, they will be quieted. Then hasten to fetch some of the water of life before the clock strikes twelve, else the door will shut again, and thou wilt be imprisoned."

The prince thanked him, took the wand and the bread, and set out on his way. When he arrived, everything was as the dwarf had said. The door sprang open at the third stroke of the wand, and when he had appeased the lions with the bread, he entered the castle, and came to a large and splendid hall, wherein sat some enchanted princes whose rings he drew off their fingers. A sword and a loaf of bread were lying there, which he carried away. After this, he entered a chamber, in which was a beautiful maiden who rejoiced when she saw him, kissed him, and told him that he had delivered her, and should have the whole of her kingdom, and that if he would return in a year their wedding should be celebrated. Likewise she told him where the spring of the water of life was, and that he was to hasten and draw some of it before the clock struck twelve. Then he went onwards, and at last entered a room where there was a beautiful newly-made bed, and as he was very weary, he felt inclined to rest a little. So he lay down and fell asleep.

When he awoke, it was striking a quarter to twelve. He sprang up in a fright, ran to the spring, drew some water in a cup which stood near, and hastened away. But just as he was passing through the iron door, the clock struck twelve, and the door fell to with such violence that it carried away a piece of his heel. He, however, rejoicing at having obtained the water of life, went homewards, and again passed the dwarf. When the latter saw the sword and the loaf, he said, "With these thou hast won great wealth; with the sword thou canst slay whole armies, and the bread will never come to an end."

But the prince would not go home to his father without his brothers, and said, "Dear dwarf, canst thou not tell me where my two brothers are? They went out before I did in search of the water of life, and have not returned."

"They are imprisoned between two mountains," said the dwarf. "I have condemned them to stay there, because they were so haughty." Then the prince begged until the dwarf released them; but he warned him, however, and said, "Beware of them, for they have bad hearts."

When his brothers came, he rejoiced, and told them how things had gone with him: that he had found the water of life and had brought a cupful away with him; and that he had rescued a beautiful princess, who was willing to wait a year for him; and that their wedding was to be celebrated and he would obtain a great kingdom.

After that they rode on together, and chanced upon a land where war and famine reigned, and whose ruler thought he must perish for scarcity of food. Then the prince went to him and gave him the loaf, wherewith he fed and satisfied the whole of his kingdom. And the prince also gave him the sword, wherewith he slew the hosts of his enemies and could now live in rest and peace. The prince then took back his loaf and his sword, and the three brothers rode on.

But after this they entered two more countries where war and famine reigned and each time the prince gave his loaf and his sword to the rulers to deliver their kingdoms. And after that they went on board a ship and sailed over the sea. During the passage, the two eldest conversed apart and said, "The youngest has found the water of life, not we. And for that our father will give him the kingdom, which belongs to us; and he will rob us of all our fortune." They then began to seek revenge, and plotted with each other to destroy him. They waited until they found him fast asleep, then they poured the water of life out of the cup, and took it for themselves, but into the cup they poured salt sea-water. Now therefore, when they arrived home, the youngest took his cup to the sick King in order that he might drink out of it, and be cured. But scarcely had he drunk a very little of the salt sea-water than he became still worse than before. And as he was lamenting over this, the two eldest brothers came, and accused the youngest of having intended

"Dear dwarf, canst thou not tell me where my two brothers are?"

to poison him, and said that they had brought him the true water of life, and handed it to him. He had scarcely tasted it, when he felt his sickness departing, and became strong and healthy as in the days of his youth.

After that they both mocked the youngest, saying, "You certainly found the water of life, but you have had the pain, and we the gain. You should have been sharper, and should have kept your eyes open. We took it from you while you were asleep at sea, and when a year is over, one of us will go and fetch the beautiful princess. But beware that you do not disclose aught of this to our father. Indeed, he does not trust you, and if you say a single word, you shall lose your life into the bargain; but if you keep silent, you shall have it as a gift."

The old King was angry with his youngest son, and thought he had plotted against his life. So he summoned the court together and had sentence pronounced upon him, that he should be secretly shot. And once when the prince was riding forth to the chase, suspecting no evil, the King's huntsman rode with him. And when they were quite alone in the forest, the huntsman looked so sorrowful that the prince said to him, "Dear huntsman, what ails you?"

The huntsman said, "I cannot tell you, and yet I ought."

Then the prince said, "Say openly what it is, I will pardon you."

"Alas!" said the huntsman, "I am to shoot you dead. The King has ordered me to do it."

Then the prince was shocked, and said, "Dear huntsman, let me live; there, I give you my royal garments; give me your common ones in their stead."

The huntsman said, "I will willingly do that; indeed, I should not have been able to shoot you." Then they exchanged clothes, and the huntsman returned home; the prince, however, went further into the forest.

After a time three wagons of gold and precious stones came to the King for his youngest son, which were sent by the three kings who had slain their enemies with the prince's sword, and fed their people with his bread, and who wished to show their gratitude for it. The old King then thought, "Can my son have been innocent?" and said to his people, "Would that he were still alive, how it grieves me that I have suffered him to be killed!"

"He still lives," said the huntsman. "I could not find it in my heart to carry out your command," and told the King how it had happened. Then a stone fell from the King's heart, and he had it proclaimed in every country that his son might return and be taken into favor again.

The princess, however, had a road made up to her palace which was quite bright and golden, and told her people that whosoever came riding straight along it to her, would be the right wooer and was to be admitted, and whoever rode by the side of it, was not the right one, and was not to be admitted. As the time was now close at hand, the eldest thought he would hasten to go to the King's daughter, and give himself out as her deliverer, and thus win her for his bride, and the kingdom to boot. Therefore he rode forth, and when he arrived in front of the palace, and saw the splendid golden road, he thought, it would be a sin and a shame if he were to ride over that, and turned aside, and rode on the right side of it. But when he came to the door, the servants told him that he was not the right man, and was to go away again.

Soon after this the second prince set out, and when he came to the golden road, and his horse had put one foot on it, he thought, it would be a sin and a shame to tread a piece of it off, and he turned aside and rode on the left side of it, and when he reached the door, the attendants told him he was not the right one, and he was to go away again.

When at last the year had entirely expired, the third son likewise wished to ride out of the forest to his beloved, and with her forget his sorrows. So he set out and thought of her so incessantly, and wished to be with her so much, that he never noticed the golden road at all. So his horse rode onwards up the middle of it, and when he came to the door, it was opened and the princess received him with joy, and said he was her deliverer, and lord of the kingdom, and their wedding was celebrated with great rejoicing.

When it was over she told him that his father invited him to come to him, and had forgiven him. So he rode thither, and told him everything: how his brothers had betrayed him, and how he had nevertheless kept silence. The old King wished to punish them, but they had put to sea, and never came back as long as they lived.

SLEEPING BEAUTY

A long time ago there were a King and Queen who said every day, "Ah, if only we had a child!" but they never had one. But it happened that once when the Queen was bathing, a frog crept out of the water onto the land, and said to her, "Your wish shall be fulfilled; before a year has gone by, you shall have a daughter."

What the frog had said came true, and the Queen had a little girl who was so pretty that the King could not contain himself for joy, and ordered a great feast. He invited not only his kindred, friends and acquaintance, but also the Wise Women, in order that they might be kind and well-disposed towards the child. There were thirteen of them in his kingdom, but, as he had only twelve golden plates for them to eat out of, one of them had to be left at home.

The feast was held with all manner of splendor and when it came to an end the Wise Women bestowed their magic gifts upon the baby: one gave virtue, another beauty, a third riches, and so on with everything in the world that one can wish for.

When eleven of them had made their promises, suddenly, the thirteenth came in. She wished to avenge herself for not having been invited, and without greeting, or even looking at any one, she cried with a loud voice, "The King's daughter shall in her fifteenth year prick herself with a spindle, and fall down dead." And, without saying a word more, she turned round and left the room.

They were all shocked; but the twelfth, whose good wish still remained unspoken, came forward, and as she could not undo the evil sentence, but only soften it, she said, "It shall not be death, but a deep sleep of a hundred years, into which the princess shall fall."

The King, who would fain keep his dear child from the misfortune, gave orders that every spindle in the whole kingdom should be burnt. Meanwhile the gifts of the Wise Women were plenteously fulfilled on the young girl, for she was so beautiful, modest, good-natured, and wise, that everyone who saw her was bound to love her.

It happened that on the very day when she was fifteen years old, the King and Queen were not at home, and the maiden was left in the palace

The king could not contain himself for joy

quite alone. So she went round into all sorts
of places, looked into rooms and
bedchambers just as she liked,
and at last came to an old
tower. She climbed up the
narrow winding-staircase, and
reached a little door. A rusty
key was in the lock, and when
she turned it the door sprang
open, and there in a little
room sat an old woman
with a spindle, busily
spinning her flax.

   "Good day, old
dame," said the King's
daughter; "what are you
doing there?"

   "I am spinning,"
said the old woman,
and nodded her head.

   "What sort of
thing is that, that rattles
round so merrily?" said
the girl, and she took

Suddenly, the thirteenth came in

the spindle and wanted to spin too. But scarcely had she touched the spindle
when the magic decree was fulfilled, and she pricked her finger with it.

   And, in the very moment when she felt the prick, she fell down upon the
bed that stood there, and lay in a deep sleep. And this sleep extended over the
whole palace; the King and Queen who had just come home and entered the
great hall, began to go to sleep, and the whole of the court with them. The
horses, too, went to sleep in the stable, the dogs in the yard, the pigeons upon
the roof, the flies on the wall; even the fire that was flaming on the hearth
became quiet and slept; the roast meat left off frizzling, and the cook, who
was just going to pull the hair of the scullery boy because he had forgotten
something, let him go and went to sleep. And the wind fell, and on the trees
before the castle not a leaf moved again.

But round about the castle there began to grow a hedge of thorns, which every year became higher, and at last grew close up round the castle and all over it, so that there was nothing of it to be seen, not even the flag upon the roof. But the story of the beautiful sleeping "Briar-Rose" (for so the princess was named) went about the country, so that from time to time kings' sons came and tried to get through the thorny hedge into the castle.

But they found it impossible, for the thorns held fast together as though they had hands, and the youths were caught in them, could not get loose again, and died a miserable death.

After long, long years a king's son came again to that country, and heard an old man talking about the thorn-hedge, and that a castle was said to stand behind it in which a wonderfully beautiful princess named Briar-Rose had been asleep for a hundred years; and that the King and Queen and the whole court were asleep likewise. He had heard, too, from his grandfather, that many kings' sons had already come, and had tried to get through the thorny

Round about the castle there began to grow a hedge of thorns,
which every year became higher

"I am not afraid, I will go and see the beautiful Briar-Rose."

hedge, but they had remained stuck fast in it, and had died a pitiful death. Then the youth said, "I am not afraid, I will go and see the beautiful Briar-Rose." The good old man tried to dissuade him as best he could, but the youth would not listen to his words.

But by this time the hundred years had just passed, and the day had come when Briar-Rose was to awake again. When the King's son came near to the thorn-hedge, it bloomed large and beautiful flowers, which parted from each other of their own accord and let him pass unhurt, before closing again behind him like a hedge. In the castle-yard he saw the horses and the spotted hounds lying asleep; on the roof sat the pigeons with their heads under their wings. And when he entered the house, the flies were asleep upon the wall. The cook in the kitchen was still holding out his hand to seize the boy, and the maid was sitting by the black hen which she was going to pluck.

He went on farther, and in the great hall he saw the whole of the court lying asleep, and up by the throne lay the King and Queen.

Then he went on still farther, and all was so quiet that a breath could be heard, and at last he came to the tower, and opened the door into the little room where Briar-Rose was sleeping. There she lay, so beautiful that he could not turn his eyes away; and he stooped down and gave her a kiss. But as soon as he kissed her, Briar-Rose opened her eyes and awoke, and looked at him quite sweetly.

Then they went down together, and the King awoke, and the Queen, and the whole court, and looked at each other in great astonishment. And the horses in the courtyard stood up and shook themselves; the hounds jumped up and wagged their tails; the pigeons upon the roof pulled out their heads from under their wings, looked round, and flew into the open country; the flies on the wall crept again; the fire in the kitchen burned up and flickered and cooked the meat; the joint began to turn and frizzle again, and the cook gave the boy such a box on the ear that he screamed, and the maid plucked the fowl ready for the spit.

And then the marriage of the King's son with Briar-Rose was celebrated with all splendor, and they lived contented to the end of their days.

DOCTOR KNOWALL

There was once on a time a poor peasant named Crabb, who drove with two oxen a load of wood to the town, and sold it to a doctor for two thalers. When the money was being counted out to him, it so happened that the doctor was sitting at table, and when the peasant saw how daintily he ate and drank, his heart desired what he saw, and he would willingly have been a doctor too. So he remained standing a while, and at length inquired if he too could not be a doctor.

"Oh, yes," said the doctor, "that is soon managed."

"What must I do?" asked the peasant.

"In the first place buy thyself an A-B-C book of the kind which has a cock on the frontispiece: in the second, turn thy cart and thy two oxen into money, and get thyself some clothes, and whatsoever else pertains to medicine; thirdly, have a sign painted for thyself with the words, 'I am Doctor Knowall,'" and have that nailed up above thy house-door."

The peasant did everything that he had been told to do.

When he had doctored people awhile, but not long, a rich and great lord had some money stolen. Then he was told about Doctor Knowall who lived in such and such a village, and must know what had become of the money. So the lord had the horses put in his carriage, drove out to the village, and asked Crabb if he were Doctor Knowall? Yes, he was, he said. Then he was to go with him and bring back the stolen money. "Oh, yes, but Grethe, my wife, must go too." The lord was willing and let both of them have a seat in the carriage, and they all drove away together.

When they came to the nobleman's castle, the table was spread, and Crabb was told to sit down and eat. "Yes, but my wife, Grethe, too," said he, and he seated himself with her at the table. And when the first servant came with a dish of delicate fare, the peasant nudged his wife, and said, "Grethe, that was the first," meaning that was the servant who brought the first dish. The servant, however, thought he intended by that to say, "That is the first thief," and as he actually was so, he was terrified, and said to his comrade outside, "The doctor knows all: we shall fare ill, he said I was the first."

There was once on a time a poor peasant named Crabb, who drove with two oxen a load of wood to the town, and sold it to a doctor for two thalers

The second did not want to go in at all, but was forced. So when he went in with his dish, the peasant nudged his wife, and said, "Grethe, that is the second." This servant was just as much alarmed, and he got out.

The third did not fare better, for the peasant again said, "Grethe, that is the third."

The fourth had to carry in a dish that was covered, and the lord told the doctor that he was to show his skill, and guess what was beneath the cover. The doctor looked at the dish, had no idea what to say, and cried, "Ah, poor Crabb." When the lord heard that, he cried, "There! he knows it, he knows who has the money!"

On this the servants looked terribly uneasy, and made a sign to the doctor that they wished him to step outside for a moment. When therefore he went out, all four of them confessed to him that they had stolen the money, and said that they would willingly restore it and give him a heavy sum into the bargain, if he would not denounce them, for if he did they would be hanged. They led him to the spot where the money was concealed.

With this the doctor was satisfied, and returned to the hall, sat down to the table, and said, "My lord, now will I search in my book where the gold is hidden." The fifth servant, however, crept into the stove to hear if the doctor knew still more. The Doctor, however, sat still and opened his A-B-C book, turned the pages backwards and forwards, and looked for the cock. As he could not find it immediately he said, "I know you are there, so you had better show yourself." Then the fellow in the stove thought that the doctor meant him, and full of terror, sprang out, crying, "That man knows everything!" Then Dr. Knowall showed the count where the money was, but did not say who had stolen it, and received from both sides much money in reward, and became a renowned man.

❦

THE GOOSE-GIRL

There was, once upon a time, an old Queen whose husband had been dead for many years, and she had a beautiful daughter. When the princess grew up she was betrothed to a prince who lived at a great distance. When the time came for her to be married, and she had to journey forth into the

distant kingdom, the aged Queen packed up for her many costly vessels of
silver and gold, and trinkets also of gold and silver, and cups and jewels—in
short, everything which appertained to a royal dowry, for she loved her child
with all her heart. She likewise sent her maid in waiting, who was to ride
with her, and hand her over to the bridegroom, and each had a horse for the
journey, but the horse of the King's daughter was called Falada, and could
speak. So when the hour of parting had come, the aged mother went into her
bedroom, took a small knife and cut her finger with it until it bled, then she
held a white handkerchief to it into which she let three drops of blood fall,
gave it to her daughter and said, "Dear child, preserve this carefully, it will be
of service to you on your way."

So they took a sorrowful leave of each other; the princess put the piece
of cloth in her bosom, mounted her horse, and then went away to her bridegroom. After she had ridden for a while she felt a burning thirst, and said
to her waiting-maid, "Dismount, and take my cup which thou hast brought
with thee for me, and get me some water from the stream, for I should like
to drink."

"If you are thirsty," said the waiting-maid, "get off your horse yourself,
and lie down and drink out of the water. I don't choose to be your servant."
So in her great thirst the princess alighted, bent down over the water in
the stream and drank, and was not allowed to drink out of the golden cup.
Then she said, "Ah, Heaven!" and the three drops of blood answered, "If thy
mother knew, her heart would break." But the King's daughter was humble,
said nothing, and mounted her horse again.

She rode some miles further, but the day was warm, the sun scorched
her, and she was thirsty once more, and when they came to a stream of
water, she again cried to her waiting-maid, "Dismount, and give me some
water in my golden cup," for she had long ago forgotten the girl's ill words.
But the waiting-maid said still more haughtily, "If you wish to drink, drink
as you can. I don't choose to be your maid." Then in her great thirst the
King's daughter alighted, bent over the flowing stream, wept and said,
"Ah, Heaven!" and the drops of blood again replied, "If thy mother knew
this, her heart would break." And as she was thus drinking and leaning right
over the stream, the handkerchief with the three drops of blood fell out
of her bosom, and floated away with the water without her observing it,
so great was her trouble.

The waiting-maid, however, had seen it, and she rejoiced to think that she had now power over the bride, for since the princess had lost the drops of blood, she had become weak and powerless. So now when she wanted to mount her horse again, the one that was called Falada, the waiting-maid said, "Falada is more suitable for me, and my nag will do for thee" and the princess had to be content with that. Then the waiting-maid, with many hard words, bade the princess exchange her royal apparel for her own shabby clothes; and at length she was compelled to swear by the clear sky above her, that she would not say one word of this to any one at the royal court, and if she had not taken this oath she would have been killed on the spot. But Falada saw all this, and observed it well.

The waiting-maid now mounted Falada, and the true bride the bad horse, and thus they traveled onwards, until at length they entered the royal palace. There were great rejoicings over her arrival, and the prince sprang forward to meet her, lifted the waiting-maid from her horse, and thought she was his consort. She was conducted upstairs, but the real princess was left standing below. Then the old King looked out of the window and saw her standing in the courtyard, and how dainty and delicate and beautiful she was, and instantly went to the royal apartment, and asked the bride about the girl she had with her who was standing down below in the courtyard, and who she was? "I picked her up on my way for a companion; give the girl something to work at, that she may not stand idle."

But the old King had no work for her, and knew of none, so he said, "I have a little boy who tends the geese, she may help him." The boy was called Conrad, and the true bride had to help him to tend the geese. Soon afterwards the false bride said to the young King, "Dearest husband, I beg you to do me a favor." He answered, "I will do so most willingly." "Then send for the knacker, and have the head of the horse on which I rode here cut off, for it vexed me on the way." In reality, she was afraid that the horse might tell how she had behaved to the King's daughter.

Then she succeeded in making the King promise that it should be done, and the faithful Falada was to die; this came to the ears of the real princess, and she secretly promised to pay the knacker a piece of gold if he would perform a small service for her. There was a great dark-looking gateway in the town, through which morning and evening she had to pass with the geese: would he be so good as to nail up Falada's head on it, so that she might see him again, more than once. The knacker's man promised to do that, and cut off the head, and nailed it fast beneath the dark gateway.

Early in the morning, when she and Conrad drove out their flock beneath this gateway, she said in passing,

"Alas, Falada, hanging there!"

Then the head answered,

Alas, young Queen, how ill you fare!
If this your tender mother knew,
Her heart would surely break in two.

Then they went still further out of the town, and drove their geese into the country. And when they had come to the meadow, she sat down and unbound her hair which was like pure gold, and Conrad saw it and delighted in its brightness, and wanted to pluck out a few hairs. Then she said,

Blow, blow, thou gentle wind, I say,
Blow Conrad's little hat away,
And make him chase it here and there,
Until I have braided all my hair,
And bound it up again.

And there came such a violent wind that it blew Conrad's hat far away across country, and he was forced to run after it. When he came back she had finished combing her hair and was putting it up again, and he could not get any of it. Then Conrad was angry, and would not speak to her, and thus they watched the geese until the evening, and then they went home.

Next day when they were driving the geese out through the dark gateway, the maiden said,

"Alas, Falada, hanging there!"

Falada answered,

Blow, blow, thou gentle wind, I say,
Blow Conrad's little hat away,

> Alas, young Queen, how ill you fare!
> If this your tender mother knew,
> Her heart would surely break in two.

And she sat down again in the field and began to comb out her hair, and Conrad ran and tried to clutch it, so she said in haste,

> Blow, blow, thou gentle wind, I say,
> Blow Conrad's little hat away,
> And make him chase it here and there,
> Until I have braided all my hair,
> And bound it up again.

Then the wind blew, and blew his little hat off his head and far away, and Conrad was forced to run after it, and when he came back, her hair had been put up a long time, and he could get none of it, and so they looked after their geese till evening came.

But in the evening after they had got home, Conrad went to the old King, and said, "I won't tend the geese with that girl any longer!"

"Why not?" inquired the aged King. "Oh, because she vexes me the whole day long."

Then the aged King commanded him to relate what it was that she did to him. And Conrad said, "In the morning when we pass beneath the dark gateway with the flock, there is a sorry horse's head on the wall, and she says to it,

> "Alas, Falada, hanging there!"

And the head replies,

> Alas, young Queen, how ill you fare!
> If this your tender mother knew,
> Her heart would surely break in two.

And Conrad went on to relate what happened on the goose pasture, and how when there he had to chase his hat.

The aged King commanded him to drive his flock out again next day, and as soon as morning came, he placed himself behind the dark gateway, and heard how the maiden spoke to the head of Falada, and then he too went into the country, and hid himself in the thicket in the meadow. There he soon saw with his own eyes the goose-girl and the goose-boy bringing their flock, and how after a while she sat down and unplaited her hair, which shone with radiance.

> Blow, blow, thou gentle wind, I say,
> Blow Conrad's little hat away,
> And make him chase it here and there,
> Until I have braided all my hair,
> And bound it up again.

Then came a blast of wind and carried off Conrad's hat, so that he had to run far away, while the maiden quietly went on combing and plaiting her hair, all of which the King observed. Then, quite unseen, he went away, and when the goose-girl came home in the evening, he called her aside, and asked why she did all these things. "I may not tell you that, and I dare not lament my sorrows to any human being, for I have sworn not to do so by the heaven which is above me; if I had not done that, I should have lost my life." He urged her and left her no peace, but he could draw nothing from her. Then said he, "If thou wilt not tell me anything, tell thy sorrows to the iron-stove there," and he went away.

Then she crept into the iron-stove, and began to weep and lament, and emptied her whole heart, and said, "Here am I deserted by the whole world, and yet I am a King's daughter, and a false waiting-maid has by force brought me to such a pass that I have been compelled to put off my royal apparel, and she has taken my place with my bridegroom, and I have to perform menial service as a goose-girl. If my mother did but know that, her heart would break."

The aged King, however, was standing outside by the pipe of the stove, and was listening to what she said, and heard it. Then he came back again, and bade her come out of the stove. And royal garments were placed on her, and it was marvelous how beautiful she was! The aged King summoned his son, and revealed to him that he had got the false bride who was only

"Alas, Falada, hanging there!"

a waiting-maid, but that the true one was standing there, as the sometime goose-girl.

The young King rejoiced with all his heart when he saw her beauty and youth, and a great feast was made ready to which all the people and all good friends were invited. At the head of the table sat the bridegroom with the King's daughter at one side of him, and the waiting-maid on the other, but the waiting-maid was blinded, and did not recognize the princess in her dazzling array. When they had eaten and drunk, and were merry, the aged King asked the waiting-maid as a riddle, what a person deserved who had behaved in such and such a way to her master, and at the same time related the whole story, and asked what sentence such an one merited?

Then the false bride said, "She deserves no better fate than to be stripped entirely naked, and put in a barrel which is studded inside with pointed nails, and two white horses should be harnessed to it, which will drag her along through one street after another, till she is dead."

"It is thou," said the aged King, "and thou hast pronounced thine own sentence, and thus shall it be done unto thee." And when the sentence had been carried out, the young King married his true bride, and both of them reigned over their kingdom in peace and happiness.

❧

3 1901 05471 8608